In love with the connect 2

Ebony Diamonds

Chapter 11

Bella

This what happens when I think 'bout you, I get in my feelings yeah, I start reminiscing yeah, next time around fuck I want it to be different yeah.

I nodded my head to Bryson' Tillers Exchange coming from the radio as I sat in the living room. I thought about the innocent lives I had taken, and I was sick about the shit. I should have paid closer attention and I would have seen that wasn't Domo fucking in our bed; it was Lando and Lex.

Lord please save her for me...

I sang along as I contemplated what the hell I was going to do. I didn't know how Domo would react to those dead bodies in the bed, and one being his friend. I decided to just leave and pretend I was never there. I got up and walked to the door, but it was too late. Domo came in with another one of his friends Drake, and they were carrying boxes with ribbons wrapped around them.

"Baby, what you doing here? You done fucked up your surprise. Where's Lex and Lando? They were supposed to be decorating for me."

I didn't say anything; I just went and wrapped my arms around his neck. "I'm sorry baby, I thought he was you and I just went off."

He looked confused and concerned all at the same time. "What the fuck did you do, Bella?"

I pointed upstairs, and he and Drake went up.

"FUCK!" I heard Domo say.

"Oh shit, he still alive nigga!"

I was relieved, but still fucked up because that meant Lex was dead. Domo came downstairs and pulled me into the kitchen.

"So you were gonna kill me, huh?" I got so scared because of the look in his eyes.

"I thought you was fuckin' Lex, baby, I just lost it." He slammed his fist down on the counter and I jumped.

"When the ambulance and police get here, tell them we found them like that, you hear me!" he yelled, and then walked off. I fucked up bad.

"Baby, please don't be mad at me; you would have done the same thing." He stopped walking down the hall and turned to me.

"I would never take your life from you."

He walked off and kicked one of the boxes they had brought in. I went and looked at it and it read *Happy birthday to my beautiful wife.* He was setting up a fucking birthday party for me because my birthday was tomorrow. I didn't even notice the streamers and shit all around the living room. I was even worse off; I thought he was fucking around again when he was just trying to do some shit for my ass.

I sat on the couch waiting for the police to come, and when they did I was so scared I felt it starting to show. The officer asked if I was ok, and I said it was the pregnancy.

"Are you sure? We can have you checked out by the EMT's, Mrs. Birkdale."

I shook my head no. "I'm fine, I guess I'm just a little rattled about this whole situation." He nodded and started asking me questions.

Domo was talking to another detective, and he stared me

down the whole time. I had this sinking feeling that just couldn't be shaken.

"Ok, we have everything we need for now; call us if you hear anything," the detective said, handing me his card. After five hours, I watched all the police walk out and I saw the coroners bringing down Lex's body. They took Lando to the hospital as soon as they got here. I was left alone with Domo and Drake.

"Ay, go up to the hospital and call me if he wakes up. If he do, make sure nobody talk to him, aight?" Domo said to Drake; Drake nodded his head, looked at me, then walked out.

"You know you fucked up, right? Lando ain't been shit but a loyal nigga to me."

I put my face in my hands and breathed heavily. "I'm sorry, Domo; I just lost it. You told me you weren't going to do that shit to me anymore, and when I saw that...I just lost my head."

He was just looking at me, and it was making me very uncomfortable. He walked out the living room and started ripping shit down off the walls. He came back and took down all the streamers and started throwing shit away.

"Look, I need to take you home. I got some shit to handle and I'm a little pissed off at you and don't want to say some shit I would regret."

I got up and stormed past him. "I can take myself home. As a matter of fact, I can go where the fuck I want. Since you Mr. fucking perfect all of a sudden and forget the bullshit you do."

I opened the door, and like lightening he came and slammed it. I jumped back trying not to get my foot caught in the door.

"Keep fucking playing with me Bella, and watch me fuck your ass up. I told you I was taking you home, and that's what the fuck I'm doing. I keep telling you to watch your mouth when you talk to me; you still don't know who the fuck I am out here, huh? Get your bag and let's go. NOW!"

I grabbed my purse off the table and walked to the car. He opened the door for me, and I slid in. I felt a tear slide down my cheek and quickly wiped it away. I saw him watching me the whole time he walked around the car to get to the driver's side.

"Are you hungry?" he asked when he started his car. I shook my head no. "Bella, you can be mad about what I said all day, but the shit stands. Stop popping off on me like I'm some low-level ass nigga you can talk that shit to. I love your ass, but you need to stop trying to run from me every time we have a disagreement. You always gonna be my wife shawty, regardless, so just let me take you to feed you and our baby, and then I can take you home," he said as he stroked the side of my face, wiping away the tear that escaped.

"Ok Domo, but you still don't have to yell at me like that."

He smacked his lips and drove off. "Damn women," he mumbled.

We stopped at Fatburger, and he got me a double bacon and some fries. I ate it on the way home and he watched me enjoy the hell out of it. He rubbed my stomach the whole drive, and the baby was kicking like crazy. When we got home, he came around and let me out the car.

"Go get some rest baby, and try to get that shit out your head. It's gonna fuck with you for a minute, but I don't want you to stress yourself or the baby. Daddy gonna handle it, aight?"

He gave me a big kiss on the lips, got back in the car, and drove away. I went inside and just walked up the steps, then crashed on the bed. I was so hurt by what I did that it consumed my thoughts. Even when I tried to watch TV, I couldn't get the visions out of my head. I couldn't stop seeing their bodies jumping from the bullets ripping through them, and all the blood.

I checked my phone to see if I missed any calls or messages. I had a dozen from my father, and just as many from Peaches. I wasn't mad they was fucking; it's just they could have said something. Now I had Bizzy hitting me up about Domo and shit. I almost forgot about all that. I meant to tell Domo. I called him, but it went to voicemail. I hated when he did that. I called my father, but he didn't answer either. I decided to just call Peaches to tell her what Bizzy was saying. She answered on the first ring.

"Bella, please don't be mad at me. It just happened." I rolled my eyes because nothing just happens.

"That's not why I'm calling. Bizzy called me right before I came to your house saying he was going to kill you and Domo. He saw Domo's car and thought it was him. You need to talk to him." I could hear a guy's voice in the background. I didn't recognize it, though.

"I'm not tripping off him. He had some bitch in there the day I moved my shit out. So fuck him."

"No, it's not fuck him. He thinks Domo's fucking you. You need to tell him otherwise because if he comes at my nigga over you, then we got an issue," I stated very seriously.

"Damn Bella, that nigga done turned you gangsta, huh? Well, I'm gonna try to get to him. Anyway, what are you doing? Can I come by so we can talk?"

I thought about telling her about what happened at the house, but I changed my mind. "I'm not feeling good; we can get up tomorrow," I said, flipping the channels.

"Well I'm coming now. You know you can't stay mad forever, so let's just speed up the process. Be there in fifteen," and she hung up.

I sat there waiting for her to come, and in exactly fifteen minutes she was ringing the doorbell. I swung the door open and just walked off. She had the kids with her, so I went and grabbed them some juice boxes out the refrigerator.

"I'm listening," I said as I sat on a stool at the breakfast bar.

"Ok; after that shit happened with Drew, I saw your pops

with Minchie…you know him, Dana's baby's father." I nodded my head yes. "Well, we started talking and laughing, and he asked for my number and I gave it to him. I didn't think it would be nothing, Bella; but he is so sweet and…" I put my hand up.

"My father is damn near fifty, Peaches. I'm just mad you didn't tell me. I had to see my father fucking my best friend. I mean, what the fuck would you be feeling?"

She threw her hands up like she was defeated. "I mean, if you really want to know, he got a long ass dick," she said, bouncing and sticking her tongue out."

I scrunched up my face. "Bitch, get out; don't nobody want to hear about that shit. Nasty ass heffa."

She was laughing, and I couldn't help but do the same. "Can you still be my bestie?" she scooted next to me and laid her head on my shoulder.

"Now why the fuck would I cut you off? I think it's nasty as fuck, but that's y'all shit."

She smiled and kissed my cheek. "That's why I love you; always loyal and understanding."

I rolled my eyes. "Whatever; what y'all doing anyway? It's eleven at night and you got the kids out."

She shrugged her shoulders. "Nothing. I just wanted to come talk to you. I'm about to head back home in a second. I just wanted to make sure I still had my best bitch by my side."

I smirked and pushed her away. "Don't think I'm going to call you Mommy, bitch. That shit dead."

She busted out laughing and got up. "Give me a hug, girl."

I stood up and hugged her. "Let me try to get some sleep." I walked to the door and let them out.

"Aight, Bella; call me tomorrow," Peaches said as she loaded the kids in the car. I closed the door and went back upstairs. I saw my phone flashing and quickly grabbed it, hoping it was Domo. It was my father. I decided to just call him back in the morning. I had a long ass day and just wanted to sleep.

****

When I woke up, Domo wasn't beside me. I immediately got angry and called his phone.

"Yeah woman," I heard his voice, but not through the phone; his voice came from the hallway. The room door opened, and he was carrying a tray of food to the bed. His phone was still ringing, so I hung up the call.

"I thought you didn't come home."

He shook his head and placed the food on the bed. It was scrambled eggs, blueberry pancakes, and sausage links. "Damn, a nigga can't get no credit, huh? Good morning to you too." He kissed me on the lips and I smiled at him.

"Thanks, baby; this looks bomb. Satia must be here." I looked at the time and it was one o'clock. I must have been drained.

"Yeah, but I cooked this for you. I hoped it would bring a smile to that pretty face of yours." He had me blushing.

"You're not eating?"

He kissed my cheek. "No, not really hungry. I got somewhere to be," he said, grabbing his towel as he got ready to get in the shower.

"Oh, I forgot to tell you. Bizzy called me yesterday and said he was going to kill you because he thought that you were fucking Peaches since my father had your car. They fucking, by the way. Peaches and my father, I mean."

He had a disturbed look on his face. "Fuck that other shit; this nigga Bizzy said what? He calling my wife and making threats? His ass is got," he said, going through his phone and tapping some keys. I guess he was sending a text. "I gotta roll; don't worry about that nigga, he know who the fuck I am."

"I wanna go; don't leave me in here again."

He grinned. "Finish eating and you can go. It's a meeting, so don't start complaining when you get bored."

I was so happy to just be getting the hell out that I didn't care. I scarfed my food down and went to join him in the shower. He had one hand on the wall as the water came down his back. He looked so sexy; I got in and started kissing his back. He turned around and put his arms over my shoulder.

"You ok, babe? You looked stressed." He ran his hand down my back to my ass, and squeezed.

"Yeah mami, I'm good. I got a lot of shit going on with the business, and I needed Lando to do some shit for me but I gotta get Drake on it, and I don't have faith in him like I did Lando. Drake a hot head, and he just gonna fuck shit up with his attitude."

I fucked his head up with that shit I did. "Well, is it anything I can do? I know this is all my fault."

He wiped the splashing water off my face. "It's good, baby; shit straight. I just gotta meet up with my supplier in a few weeks, and I needed back up. He trying to up the price on my bricks and we got into a little confrontation over the phone, and I don't know how this nigga gonna act. I ain't scared, but I need niggas that's gonna listen before they jump off, and Drake ain't that nigga. He gonna pull the strap as soon as a nigga look at him funny."

"Did he wake up yet?" I asked, hoping he said yes.

"No, he in a coma; you nipped his heart and they had to slow his blood flow so he wouldn't bleed out. Don't worry about it. I told you daddy got this."

He soaped up my loofah and started washing over my titties. The sensation had me feeling wet and ready. He must have sensed it because he placed his hands between my legs, and started running his fingers over my clit.

"Damn, girl. You ready for the dick, huh?"

I bit my bottom lip and stood on my toes to kiss him. He came down and sucked my bottom lip into his mouth, and we were in it. He couldn't pick me up because of my stomach, so he turned me around and went in. The splashing of the water and the sounds we were creating were so sexy that I came after only a few strokes.

"Damn; you cumming on daddy dick already, huh?" He slapped my ass, and I screamed out.

"SHIT DOMO!"

He was banging my pussy out. I had to slow him down before he sent me into early labor. He stroked me like he had love coming out his dick, and my eyes were rolled into the back of my head. He took a handful of my hair and had my back arched while he dug into me like he was looking for something.

"Go get in the bed," he said, pulling out and leaving the shower running. I flew to the bed in anticipation of some more of that good dick. His phone started ringing, and I was so pissed off that he answered it.

"Man, fuck Charlene; I got a meeting, but I will be there. Don't let that nigga leave; this the last fucking time." He hung up and called somebody.

"Yeah man; head to Charlene spot and hold that nigga there 'til I get there, aight?"

Next, he threw his phone on the bed. He looked pissed off; I didn't want to ask him who Charlene was, so I just asked something simple.

"What's wrong?"

He shook his head like the person on the other end just blew his whole day. "It's always something, baby. Let's get back in and clean up. I got you later," he said. I was so pissed; I was ready to keep fucking.

"Ok, you better," I said, getting up and getting back in the shower. We got dressed and left.

The meeting was long and boring as hell; I was sitting across from Domo and listened to him and the contractors go over numbers and some other shit. I hated this shit when I was his assistant, and I hated it even more right now. Domo was a genius; he had stood to make forty million dollars for his company building this chain of hotels for these people. He had the best architects and construction crews in Miami. He didn't even have to push dope, but I guess he wanted it all. I was so happy when they signed the paperwork so we could get the fuck out of there. We walked down to the car and went to the next destination. I was anxious to find out who the hell this Charlene was.

We pulled up to an apartment building similar to the one I was living in before.

"Stay right here, aight? I need to handle some shit."

Oh shit. I thought to myself. Somebody done fucked up and he was going to do something he didn't want me to see.

"What you keep telling me, Domo? I'm the Bonnie to your Clyde, boo."

I knew he wouldn't let shit happen to me or the baby. I just wanted to be nosey, I guess.

"Aight, Griselda Jr," he said, and we laughed at his joke about me being Griselda Blanco. I hoped I didn't change that much. I guess I was just tired of being some weak little bitch, and I was loving the power I felt with Domo.

We got out and I followed him to the steps, and we walked up. He knocked on the door directly in front the step landing, and I saw somebody peek out the window.

"Open the fucking door!" he yelled, and the door swung open. There was a woman standing there with a t-shirt and underwear on; she had a busted lip and a black eye. It looked like her hair was yanked out on one side because she had a bald spot.

"Who is this?" she said, looking at me. He brushed past her and went straight to the back. When we got inside, there was a guy sitting on the bed, and Terri was standing there with a gun to the man's head. Terri was another one of his goons who I only saw when some shit was going down.

"Go sit out front, mami. Be out in a second," Domo said, and I turned and walked out.

"So, you with Domo huh? I'm Charlene, by the way." She reached her hand out to shake mine, and I shook it.

"I'm his wife."

Her eyes grew wide as I showed her my ring. "Wow; I didn't see him as being the marrying type. He usually keeps a flock of broads. How you snag him?"

This bitch was about to get on my nerves.

"Y'all use to fuck or something? You seem like you trying to start some shit with me, and it's pissing me the fuck off," I said, moving closer to her.

"I ask whatever I want about my brother."

She was his sister? Why the hell he ain't tell me that when we left?

"Oh, I ain't know that, but you still ain't gotta be all in my shit like that."

She laughed and sat on the couch. "I feel you; my brother got his ways, but he aight for the most part. He didn't even tell me he got married. That's fucked up."

He didn't tell me shit about her; come to think of it, he never told me shit about his family, except his father.

"Well, it wasn't planned. It was a last minute thing."

She sat forward and rubbed my stomach. "Damn, and you pregnant as fuck too? This nigga wrong as shit for not telling me nothing about you. I got a niece or nephew on the way and he kept the shit. He did that shit when he was with Lashay too. Their baby died though; after that, she went wild and she was fucking another nigga, and she ended up missing. I think Domo did something to her, but I never say it. He loved that girl to death and she did that nigga dirty as shit."

He didn't tell me that shit either. *Damn, what else don't I know about him?*

"What happened to the baby?"

She looked around the corner to see if Domo was coming before she answered. "This bitch was shooting dope while she was pregnant. She overdosed and it killed the baby; she lived though and that fucked him up bad. He ain't even know she was on that shit. I mean, he like to do some white, but he ain't never got bad on the shit."

Damn; she was giving me an earful. I guess that's why he never mentioned the shit because he was embarrassed.

"Damn, that's crazy. Well, he seems to be fine now. I mean, he's been good to me."

Just then, Domo walked out with the guy who was in back. His face was badly beaten, and he was being dragged.

"Oh my God, Dominic! I said talk to him."

Domo looked at her and dropped the dude on the floor. "Look man, the next time this nigga whooping your ass, call the fucking police. I'm not gonna to keep coming here for you to tell me to talk to him. Either leave his ass alone or stop calling me, man. Touch my sister again nigga, and watch me drop your ass in the dirt." Charlene ran over to check on her man.

"You ready to go, sexy?" Domo asked me. I nodded my head yes.

"It was nice meeting you," I said as Domo rushed me out the door.

"So that's your sister, huh?"

He kept his eyes straight forward, paying attention to the road. "Yeah, that's her. She don't know how to leave a nigga that beat on her and shit. To be honest, I didn't want to tell you about her because of your situation. That's why I wanted to help you so bad, because I know how fucked up the shit is when you see somebody going through it. She wouldn't listen to me, and she still won't. But you, you wanted better and I wanted to give you that. I know I did some fucked up shit, and I own that shit. I never wanted to do you like that, and I just want you to have something you never had. Love and admiration." He pulled at my heart with those words. I was so in love with this nigga right now.

"Damn; you know how to make me blush, don't you? I love you, boy," I said, rubbing my hand down his neck.

"I love you more, baby."

DOMO

A nigga had a lot on his plate now. I loved Bella to death, but she did some dumb ass shit and I didn't want to tell her how bad she fucked up, because I knew it would scare her. Lando wasn't just my right-hand man; he was my supplier's son, and that's why I wanted him to go to this meeting with me because he could talk his father down on the prices. Lando was my homie from high school before I got into this game. That's how I got hooked up with his pops; he didn't want to be on no kingpin shit, so he just rode with a nigga and it's been that way for years. His father asked me what happened to him, and I told him somebody broke into the house and did that shit. Hopefully, Lando won't remember it was Bella, because we gonna be all the way fucked up if he does. I ain't scared of the nigga; I just don't want shit to happen to my wife. I'm still not going down without taking some mufuckas with me if it gets to that point.

Drake and I got out the car to head to Mario's door. I knew I had to give this nigga a speech about not blowing his cool; we were outnumbered, and I couldn't have him fucking up.

"Look bruh, I need you to be easy; I ain't got time for the bullshit today."

He laughed me off. "I got you, Domo," I side-eyed the nigga, because I knew this was a bad idea. I didn't have nobody else because I had my muscle watching the warehouse. Some niggas plotted and failed, now I wanted to make sure everything was straight.

"Yeah, I hear you nigga; just remember what I said. Don't make me kill your ass myself." He knew I meant it too.

I hit the doorbell, and the guard opened the door. We walked to the back, and Mario was sitting on the sofa watching a porno. What type of gay shit was this? I wasn't boutta sit here and watch no porn with another grown ass man.

"Mario, we could always come back if you busy."

He flicked the remote and turned the TV off. "How are you, Domo? I see you got a replacement for my son already," he said, lighting his cigarette.

"No, I ain't replacing him. I just needed to have somebody with me, you know."

He exhaled his smoke. "You don't trust me now? I mean, I should be the one worried. My son gets shot in your house, and nobody knows nothing. Sounds funny to me, Domo."

I sat on the barstool and kept my eyes on his men. "I wouldn't have no reason to try to do my nigga dirty, you feel me? I ain't come here for this though I told you what I knew, and ain't shit gonna change about that."

"Always about business with you, Dominic. Well, let's do it then. I need twenty-five a key. Shit is hot; it's becoming more dangerous to get here, and we are taking all the risk."

"Just like I told you, I'm not paying that bullshit. Especially for some shit that may have been stepped on before I got it." He looked insulted, but I didn't give a fuck. I knew what good raw was, and that shit was cut.

"You saying I cheated you?" he asked, leaning forward.

I shrugged my shoulders. "I'm saying you need to keep our original deal, or I can take the millions I drop with you elsewhere. I mean, I heard Jay is selling them thangs for ten a key, and it's some good shit too. I'm taking a loss if I let you fuck me out of twenty-five, bruh." I saw his eyes turn cold. I got to him and I knew it was dangerous, but I ain't never had no bitch in me so I stood my ground.

"Then our arrangement is complete. You can get this last shipment, but our business is done."

I stood up and signaled for Drake to step off with me. "Been a pleasure," I said, walking out of the office.

"Dominic!" Mario called out. I stood where I was, not bothering to turn back.

"If I find out you had anything to do with my boy being shot, we're going to have more than words."

I saw Drake reach in his back, and I grabbed his arm. "Man, fuck this nigga, Domo; that nigga making threats, bruh."

"Nigga, be smart; it's at least twenty guards around here. We gonna be dead before he pull the trigger." I shook my head and answered Mario back from the hallway. "Looking forward to it," I said, and we got in the car and left.

I was bluffing, and he called it. I hated to do this, but I needed to get in contact with one of my plugs outside the country. I had to supply over one hundred dealers, and I needed the best. I pulled out my phone to call my father. He wasn't going to be happy about this shit at all. I especially couldn't tell him Bella had shot Lando. My father was ruthless, and he was what people considered America's nightmare. He didn't give a fuck what he did and who saw him do it, because he would lay them down too. He didn't answer, and I decided to just stop by. I dropped Drake off at his baby mothers house, and kept going until I reached my father's place.

I sat in the car as I answered the text Bella had sent wanting to know what time I was going to be home. I had more stops to make, so I told her it would be a few more hours. Of course, she bitched a fit; but she knew I had moves to make. She was my baby though; ever since I saw her in the store that day, I couldn't get her out my mind. Actually, it was before that. I had seen her with

Drew's bitch ass, and I always thought she was a bad joint. She gave me every reason to wanna watch that ass closely and wait for the nigga to fuck up.

Peaches been gave me the scoop on her a while back, and she didn't even know it; we were at a cookout for one of my loyals coming home from jail. She told me her father was locked up, and when I heard who he was I was like damn; the forbidden fruit. I watched her at the barbecue the whole day. I saw her and Drew arguing, and she was crying and sitting at the furthest table from the barbecue. I knew I saw her with Bizzy's girl Peaches a lot, so I asked about her and she told me all about her and Drew's bullshit. I knew how he was treating her, and I wanted to be her hero and make it easy for her to want me.

I know I did my bullshit on her, but I swear she my heart, and can't no bitch made me feel different. I even stopped snorting that shit because I wanted her to be happy, and that was one of the things I did that made her unhappy. I got her doing the shit too, and I had to think about how fucked up that was to put somebody on to some shit like that. I was doing good though; I hadn't so much as looked at another broad since the Paris shit. I wasn't going to hurt her like that again; in all honesty, it really was just business.

My father always told me to let my dick do the talking when it came to females. I'm sure I could have got easy weight for the lowest. I guess I didn't think about hurting Bella when I chose to do the shit, and for that I was a sorry ass nigga.

I heard the sprinklers come on, and it pulled me out of my phone. I forgot what the hell I was doing for a minute. I walked up to the porch, put my key in, and walked inside. I didn't think he was home because it was quiet as shit. It was actually too quiet, and it kind of alarmed me. I pulled out my phone to call him and jumped when I was touched, and he stood there looking the same way I was feeling.

"Nigga, I almost killed you. Why the fuck you ain't tell me

you were coming by?"

I smacked my lips, brushed past him, and went to the kitchen. "Your old ass ain't killing nobody. Your daughter nigga fuckin her up again." I went to the fridge and grabbed a soda.

"Yeah, keep sleeping young nigga and watch my work, boy. You wish you could be like your pops one day. Anyway, as far as Charlene, she doing the shit to herself. I been told her not to bother me with that shit if she wasn't ready to attend his funeral, so I don't want to hear it. What happened with Mario?" he asked, and I knew he was about to blow his top when I told him we lost our plug.

"He wanted twenty-five a key, Pop. I told him to fuck himself, pretty much. I ain't paying that shit. Then he talked shit about Lando getting hit."

He started rubbing his hand over his head, and I knew that meant he was heated. "You didn't even try to talk to the nigga, did you? On some real shit though, you need to tell me what happened to his kid. I would be looking at you sideways too, nigga." I wasn't about to tell him shit.

I shrugged my shoulders and drank my soda. "You know the game. Some niggas prolly ran in my shit and thought he was me or something. I don't know."

He looked at me like he knew I was lying. "Nigga, I worked too hard to build this shit for you to be fucking up now, man. You need to find a new plug, and now. Did you get in with them French niggas?"

I didn't speak to Pierre again after I killed his daughter. He didn't know we were fucking, so he didn't think of me as a suspect. I gave him my condolences and everything. I knew I had fucked up and had to fix the shit. Bella wanted the bitch dead, and I would be a hypocrite if I didn't do it. I told her anybody who touched her would die, and I guess she wanted the same from me.

"Nah, I'ma see what they talking about. I still got that

Cuban nigga too so we straight, Pops." I dapped him up, and he stopped me.

"Did you tell your wife about that bitch yet?" I shook my head no; I knew what bitch he was talking about. Lashay. What the fuck he bringing that hoe up for?

"No, fuck that bitch. She need to stay buried, man," I said, still walking to the door.

"She called me looking for you."

I stopped in my tracks and turned to him. "Why you just telling me this now?"

"Because I didn't want you to fuck up a good thing. You seem to be better with Bella, and you know Lashay ain't shit but trouble."

I knew he was right. No matter what the bitch did, I still loved her dumb ass. I would never fuck with her again, but I didn't want to be tempted to hit the pussy when she came around. I could never resist her, but for Bella's sake I would try my hardest. After our baby died and she turned into a hoe on a nigga, I told her if she didn't get as far as she could away from me I would kill her, and she left and hasn't been seen for years.

"I ain't fucking up nothing, Pops. I'ma holla at you later," I said, walking to the door.

"I been meaning to ask you something. You told Bella about that shit back in the day? You must not have because she still with you." I shook my head no. "Good; you know she a daddy's girl, and she would give the shit up to Antonio in a heartbeat." I knew he was right; that's why I never said shit.

I left thinking I was about to fuck up. I wasn't trying to do that to Bella again, so I knew it was best if I just stayed away and made no contact with Lashay. I got in the car and just went home. All the shit I had to do could wait; I needed reassurance.

Chapter 12

Bella

I was now eight months pregnant, and big as a house. I was ready to have this boy and be done with this pregnancy. Everything made me feel miserable, and all Domo's black ass would say was that it was his little man showing the world who was boss. For the life of me, I couldn't get comfortable, and I just wanted to sleep and eat all day. We had been busy decorating the nursery to make it perfect for DJ.. Yes, Dominic Jr. I know it sounds cliché, but he wanted a junior and I was happy to give him that.

I was eating ice cream and sitting in the living room when the doorbell rang. I went to look through the peephole and saw that it was my father. I only talked to him one time since the incident at Peaches' house. I opened the door and was surprised to see him with an another lady. She was older with long hair, and she was clearly Hispanic.

"Who is this?" I asked with a little bit of an attitude.

"This is Lizzy; she's a friend," he said, kissing her neck and getting me irritated.

"Can we talk for a minute?" I asked him as he walked into the foyer.

"You can sit down, mi amor." She smiled at me and had a

thick layer of lipstick over her teeth. I laughed and turned to walk to the kitchen.

"Papa, what the hell is going on? Peaches is my best friend, and I don't want to see her get played like that."

He shook his head and had a slight grin on his face. "Listen, mi Haji. You must not be as close as you think if she didn't tell you what happened; she went back to her little boyfriend, and I didn't give a fuck because it was her funeral. I don't have time for a bitch who don't know what she wants, so fuck her. Now stop being rude and come talk to us; I don't want to hear about that, what are you kids saying now? Thot, right?"

I shook my head at him using that phrase. I was so disappointed in Peaches; like oh my God, why would she go back to him? Bizzy was just as bad as Drew at one point, and now he was back to his old ways. I was scared for her, so I decided I was going to call her as soon as my father left. I went out and spoke to his new girlfriend. She was, nice but she didn't have to cake that cheap ass Dollar Tree make up on her face so hard. She looked like a damn Halloween mask. My father was a gorgeous man, and for his age his body was tight as a dude in his twenties. I pretty much figured out the reason he was with her after about an hour into the conversation. She was Colombian, and she had a plug that was better than what Domo was giving him. He was a damn gigolo.

I called Peaches right after my father left, and she didn't pick up. A second later, I got a text from her saying she didn't want to talk, and she would call me when she felt better. That was odd; no matter what mood she was in, she always wanted to talk to me. I called again, and the text she sent back made me even more suspicious.

Peaches: I'm happy and doing good.

What the fuck does that mean? I didn't even ask her that. I started to think the worst. I called anyway, and she still didn't pick up. I sat the phone down and said fuck it, and called Bizzy. He answered and acted the way I thought he would.

"What the fuck you calling my phone for?"

I exhaled like I was over his bitch ass attitude already. "I was calling trying to find Peaches."

"That bitch good; she right here minding her fucking business, and you need to do the same. Stop calling my fucking girl. She don't wanna be friends with your stank ass. Bitch," and he hung up. Bitch ass nigga.

I grabbed my keys and drove to their house. I slowly rode past to see if I could see anything. All the blinds were down. I knew Domo would be super pissed, but I had to check on her. I went to the side of the house and tried to look into the windows. I couldn't see shit. I went around back to look through the patio, and I heard Peaches talking.

"Yeah, I don't know what I'm going to do. Bizzy is threatening to tell Bella everything." I peeked around the corner and saw her talking on the phone. Her back was turned to me, so she couldn't see I was there. I was about to go around the corner until I heard her say something that stopped my heart and soul.

"Well, how would you feel knowing another one of your friends had a baby with your man?"

Wait—what man was she talking about? I started getting sweaty and shaking. I stepped on a stick, and she turned around and saw me standing there.

"So, what baby are you talking about, and with who?"

Her face was frozen, and she had her mouth partially open. "I...um. Look Bella, it wasn't like that—"

I stopped her. "Just tell me, bitch. I mean, you smile in my fucking face all the time, and now you can't even look at me?" She cut her eyes at me, and I heard the patio door slide open.

"What the fuck is this bitch doing here?" I looked at Bizzy in disgust because he was clearly drunk as shit, and sloppy wasn't even the word for how he was stumbling. He had on a dirty white tank top and a pair of shorts. I never seen him look like this; he was always handsome and dressed down.

"Fuck you, nigga! You think Domo won't lay your ass down like he did your bitch ass boy?" I could see the fire set in his eyes. He started to come toward me, but I pulled my old faithful out and he stopped in his tracks.

IN LOVE WITH THE CONNECT 2

"Bella, please just hear me out," Peaches cried out to me. Bizzy had his fist balled up like he was ready to attack. I was going to light his ass up if he took a step toward me.

"I'm listening. Matter of fact, Bizzy, let me know what you been wanting to tell me? Peaches seems to be at a loss for words all of a sudden."

"This hoe was fucking my homeboy that's why I was whipping her ass. I bet she ain't tell you that's why she left, right? I found out not too long ago that Marcus was Drew's kid. A little bit before lil' Bizzy's party. I forgave my nigga because a bitch gonna be a hoe regardless. Who would turn down free pussy?"

Peaches had tears in her eyes. I couldn't believe this bitch did that shit to me. I mean, I gave two fucks about Drew at this point, but she was my friend.

"Bitch, I'm his god mother! How the fuck you do me like that? You acted like you hated the nigga and wanted me to leave because of what he was doing to me, but whole time you just wanted him for yourself. Stupid bitch."

She wiped her tears. "I don't know what to say, Bella. I swear, I didn't mean to hurt you. We were getting high one day, and you was in the hospital after he pushed you out the window. I came to get your stuff, and he poured his heart out about how he didn't want to hurt you, and I felt bad. I mean, it just happened."

Bizzy hauled off and slapped the shit out of her, and she held her face; I didn't even feel bad. She threw a punch at him, and it landed on his jaw as he stumbled. I let them fight and walked away. I couldn't believe this bitch. I swear, if I wasn't pregnant, I would have whooped her ass myself. I got to the car and saw Peaches stumbling from the back yard, bloodied and bowled over.

I got in the car and watched Bizzy walk to her and start stomping her. I knew I was ready to beat her ass myself, but I wasn't about to let him do this. I got out and let off a shot to stop him. I saw the front door open, and Marcus and lil' Bizzy were standing in the door watching everything.

"Daddy, stop doing that," Marcus said while crying.

"I ain't your daddy, muthafucka. This bitch let any nigga nut in her, and that's how your ass got in my house."

I couldn't believe he said that to that baby. I had to get them and Peaches away from this fool.

"Peaches, come get in. Come on, babies."

The kids came running to the car. Bizzy tried to grab them, and I shot in the air again and he stopped. I kept the gun on him and he had his nostrils flared; I knew I had to get the fuck out of there before I ran out of bullets.

"Peaches, come on. Don't worry about him; he ain't that stupid." She crawled on the ground and made her way to the car.

"I got y'all bitches," Bizzy said as he ran in, looking like Red from Friday after he got his chain snatched.

"Bella, please forgive me. I mean, we always had each other's back," Peaches said as I drove away.

"Peaches, I can't deal with this shit right now. I just..." I felt the sharp pain in my stomach, and I got scared because it felt like when I miscarried.

"Bella, what's wrong?"

I tried to speak, but I was again hit with another pain. I thought I peed on myself when the water started coming from between my legs.

"Oh my God, Bella, your water broke!"

I pulled over and opened the door, and immediately bowled over in pain. I felt like I had the worse cramps a bitch could have.

"Let me drive, Bella."

I put all the bullshit aside and let her help me. I would deal with her disloyal ass later. She helped me to the car, then ran around and sped to the hospital. I pulled out my phone to call Domo and put it on speaker, because I was crushing it every time I got pain.

"THE BABY COMING!" I screamed into the phone when he answered.

"What hospital you at?" He sounded like he was panicking.

"Were going to Sanai. We pulling up now," Peaches said.

"Ok baby, be there in five seconds. I love you, girl."

"I love you too, nigga; now hurry the hell up!"

Peaches got out and grabbed a wheelchair. She was limping, and her face was fucked up. A passing EMT stopped her.

"Oh my God, ma'am; what happened?! You need the police?" She looked embarrassed; I would be too if I looked like Mayweather knocked me the fuck out.

"No, I'm fine. My friend is having a baby."

I wanted to say *bitch you barely my friend right now,* but she was trying to help and I was in no condition to be a bitch. The EMT ran inside and grabbed a technician.

"Just breath, miss; we don't want the baby to lose oxygen." I started breathing heavy and got lightheaded. Another pain hit me like a brick to the gut.

"GET THIS DAMN BABY OUT NOW!"

I was grabbing onto the tech and trying to fight through what I assumed was a contraction. They whisked me up to labor and delivery, and I wanted to pass out because of how much I was hurting. My butthole started to feel like I was trying to take a constipated shit. They moved me to a room, and the nurse sat a gown on the bed.

"I need you to change into this right away," she said, slamming the gown on the bed.

"I can't even move, how you expect me to do that?"

She picked up the gown as if she was irritated. After she helped with the gown, I was laying in the bed screaming my lungs out as she placed the monitors on my stomach.

"Ma'am, we need as much information as you can give us so we can enter you in the system," the registrar said as she came in with a rolling computer.

"AAAAAAAAHHHHHH!" I screamed; I couldn't even get the words out.

"Bella Birkdale," I heard Domo's say, and I got so happy knowing he was here. He ran over and grabbed my hand.

"Insurance?" she said as she typed my name in.

"Man, you don't see she in pain? Y'all can't do this shit

later?"

She rolled her eyes up. "We need to make sure y'all can pay for this," she said, shifting to the left with her head leaned to the side.

"Bitch, I'm Dominic Birkdale. I could buy this fucking hospital. Send a doctor in here before I air this muthafucka out."

"Domo, baby. AAAAAAAHHH." I tried to calm him down, but the baby was whooping my ass."

"Fuck her, Bella; my baby boy ready to come out."

The girl bugged her eyes out and left the room. The nurse was quiet; I guess she ain't wanna get cursed out either. She came and spread my legs, and checked my cervix.

"Ok, you're at four. It's not too late for an epidural. Do you want one?"

I nodded my head violently. I would take a hammer to the head to stop this shit. After getting my epidural, I felt better but the pressure was killing me.

"I'm Doctor Braxton. So are you ready to see your baby, guys?" he said, smiling and washing his hands. He checked my cervix again, and I was ready to push. I felt like my insides were being ripped out when Dominic Junior slid into the world, weighing 9 pounds. Four ounces. Domo was so proud; he was hogging him already. He was beautiful too; he had a full head of hair, and the cutest dimples in his cheeks. He came out dark like Domo, and I loved how much he looked like him already.

"Look what you did for me, Bella. I love you more than ever right now, boo." He kissed my forehead.

"I love you too, baby. Look at him."

I smiled as DJ.. snuggled up to Domo's chest. This moment was the most perfect time I ever had in my life. I had my own little family now.

When they moved us to a room, Peaches came in with the kids. They were in awe of the little man, and made silly faces at him the whole time. Peaches' face was swollen on the right, and she had a busted lip and bruises on her neck. No matter how fucked up she had been, I still felt sorry for her. I guess it was the victim in me that still wouldn't want to see her like this. Domo wanted to know what happened, and I told him everything except the part about her and Drew having a baby. I just felt like he didn't need to know that; he hated for me to even speak his name. He was, of course, angry I went alone because Bizzy had already threatened me, so I had to hear his speech. I felt like a fool now, though; after finding out she was a snake the whole time we were friends, it crushed me. I can't lie and say she didn't look out for me, and she was always there when I needed her; but how can you call yourself a friend and do some bullshit like that? I had to fall back from her after that shit. I hoped she didn't go back to him and would be safe but as for now our friendship was over.

Peaches

I know what I did to my friend was fucked up. I don't even know how it got to that point. I knew Drew was a piece of shit, and I still let him fuck me. I mean, the dick was just so good that I couldn't stop myself from being a trifling bitch. I had to make this shit up to Bella; she was one of the only friends I had. I had a few of my day ones, but she was special to me too. I fucked up and got pregnant at that, and when Bizzy found out he was on a rampage to make me pay. Every day he was fucking me up, and I couldn't say I didn't deserve the shit. He had fucked around on me numerous times, but he never popped up with the next bitch's baby. Still, I loved him and I wanted us to work. Things were finally getting back to normal, and he had to get that fucking test. I guess the fact that Marcus looked nothing like him triggered his imagination. I didn't know what the fuck I was going to do now. I told him the truth after he confronted me with the test that Marcus wasn't his, and that was the worst ass whooping I ever got from him; I couldn't say I didn't deserve that one, though.

After I left the hospital, I went to a hotel and tried to figure out my next move. I had dough, so that wasn't an issue; I just needed to know what to do with myself now. I wanted to get faded. I dropped the kids at my mother's house, and she was livid when she saw my face. She called the police on Bizzy, and I knew that would only fuel the rage. I left before the police could show up to get a report. I didn't want to give him any more ammunition to kill my ass.

I bought a bottle, then went to pick up some tree from my

homie Lova. She was dom, and you couldn't tell her she wasn't a nigga. The only way you would know she was a girl was because of her titties. She was a friend of mine, and we use to fuck around back in the day; every time she saw me, she would bring up our old sexual encounters and I would just laugh her off. I knew she would give me a full court press about my face, so I wanted to go and just leave as fast as possible. When I got to her corner, she was sitting there talking to some girl who looked like she was lusting with her. I smiled, knowing she was feeding her those charming lines and sexy attitude.

"Damn, what a girl gotta do to get high around here?"

She put her hand to her forehead to cover the sun so she could see who was yelling at her. She smiled when she saw it was me.

"Hey, baby girl; your fine ass need some of my good shit, huh?" I rolled my eyes as she got closer to the car.

"What the fuck happened to your face, shawty?" She looked like she was more upset than I was about it.

"You know how shit is." I went into my purse to pull out my money.

"Nah, I don't. You need me to handle that nigga or something? You can't let this nigga keep doing this shit to you."

"I'm good, Lova; can you just give me a three five?"

She shook her head, then went to the bush and grabbed a brown bag. She pulled out a baggie of tree and came back to the car.

"You need to chill with me tonight; I don't feel good about this shit."

I handed her the money. "I'm fine, Lova. I will hit you up later so you can know I'm ok."

"Aight; you better call me before I gotta come looking for that ass."

I smiled, rolled my window up, and drove off.

I sat in the room smoking one jay after the other. This shit wasn't helping at all; it just made me more paranoid, and I felt even worse than before. I had started to doze off when my phone started vibrating. It was Bizzy's ass. I knew he would be calling me soon, and I hated that I was going to answer the phone.

"What the fuck you want!" I screamed into the phone.

"You let that bitch come take you and my kids from me?"

I could tell he was even more drunk than this morning, if that was possible. Before Bella showed up earlier, he was downing forties and drinking rum since eight this morning. He should have been passed out somewhere, but I guess his anger was fueling him.

"Look Bizzy, we did this shit for years, man. I know I did my shit and you did yours, but I can't be with you no more. I'm done, so please don't call my phone no more. I can't live this way." I heard something shatter, which meant he broke something.

"Bitch, you better have your ass here or I'm killing your whole family tonight!" I sat up and immediately thought about how I dropped the kids off at my mom's house.

"Ok ok, I will be there, but my mom took the kids to Alabama to visit her sister a few hours ago."

I could hear him laughing. "That's a good bitch, and tell your old ass mother to bring my fucking kids back." He hung up, and I called my mother quickly.

"Ma, I'm sending you some money through Western Union; please take the kids and go. Bizzy talking crazy again. Take Anna and Dion too." I was referring to my brother and sister.

"See Latoya, you always getting us into some bullshit because of that man. Now I gotta up and run because you can't choose better? I swear, if anything happens to my grandbabies, I will never speak a word to your dumb ass again. Anna ain't been home since yesterday. I can't make a grown woman up and leave either."

She was really mad; she was calling me by my government name and shit. She hung up on me, and I couldn't help but agree with her. I didn't know where Anna was, but I was going to call her to see where she was at so she could roll too. I Western Unioned my mother three thousand dollars to start. I texted her to tell her to pick it up, and that I would be depositing more tomorrow in her account. She didn't even respond to me. I waited around the hotel for a while, and she finally told me they were at the airport. Thank God.

I called my sister, but she didn't answer Her lil' hot ass got on my fucking nerves. She turned eighteen a few weeks ago, and my mom had been telling me she lost her damn mind thinking she was grown. I texted her and told her to call me now. My phone started ringing; I thought I was Anna, but it was Bizzy. I hit the end button. I wasn't going back to that fool; I just didn't want to put anybody else in danger.

I called the one person who I knew I could get to come protect me—Antonio, Bella's father. I knew he was fucked up about how I left him, but after I told Bizzy it wasn't Domo but Antonio, he told me if I didn't come home and leave him that he would kill him, Bella, and anybody else I loved. I didn't want to risk it, so I broke things off and it's been a living hell ever since. I was hoping he would answer, and he did.

"Who is this?" he said, and that hurt my feelings because he must have deleted me from his contacts.

"It's me, I need you to come to the hotel on 5th. I'm in trouble and I don't know what to do." I could hear a woman in the background going off in Spanish.

"I'm kind of busy right now, mami; call your baby daddy. I'm sure he could help." I felt the tears slide down my face.

"Please." That was all I could say. He smacked his lips.

"Aight, I'm on the way."

I hung up and took another drink. I needed to calm my nerves; I knew once Bizzy realized I wasn't coming, he would be looking for me high and low. After thirty minutes, I started to think Antonio wasn't coming—that's until he texted me and asked which hotel and which room. I forgot there was like three on this block. I gave him the info, and a few minutes later he was knocking on the room door. I tried to fix myself up as much as possible. When I opened the door, he was standing there tall and bulky in his tank top. He was forty, and fine as hell. I peeped that shit when he came to the party and lit Drew's ass up. He could easily pass for twenty, and he was shitting on most of these young niggas with his looks. He had a mean look on his face when he walked in.

"He did that shit to you, right?" I forgot how my face looked for a minute.

"Yeah; I know you're going to say I told you so, but I had to go back. He threatened to kill you, Bella, and all my family—just like he did again tonight. I had to send the kids and my family away."

He shook his head. "You know I would have popped his ass. Now my girlfriend pissed at me because I came to help you out."

"You got a girlfriend now?"

He looked at me with those blue eyes and rubbed his hand down my face. "I'm not into games, sweetheart. You shoulda stayed your ass with a nigga that was doing you right. Now you lost out. I still fucks with you the long way though, so what do you need?" His accent had started to come out even more. It was sexy as shit too. I went into to try to kiss him and he stopped me.

"That's not going to happen. Tell me what you need."

"I just want you to stay with me until I can get Bizzy to leave me alone. I have to do something before he kills me," I said, feeling defeated.

"I can't do that. I have a woman now, and she won't understand it at all. Tell you what, I can send somebody to come sit with you for tonight."

I shook my head no and went to grab my purse. I was just going to leave. Maybe I could meet up with my mother and the kids if she told me where she was heading.

"I'm fine. You can go, I shouldn't have called you." I started walking out and he grabbed my arm.

"Don't be mad because you made your choices. I understand you wanted to protect us all, but you could have gone about it another way. Now sit your ass down and wait for my nigga to come through. I swear, if you not here when he come, I'm gonna get your ass myself." He was looking deep into my eyes and I was melting. He finally gave me what I wanted. He kissed me and rubbed across my ass, and I knew he was about to give me that long pipe. His phone rang and he looked at it, and rolling his eyes while answering it.

"Look, I told you I will be home when the fuck I'm there. Stop calling me." He hung up.

"I gotta go, I already hit my homie to come. Try to be safe and when you get to where you're going, call me." Fuck, I wanted some bad; shit, I needed it.

"Ok. Thanks, Antonio," I said, feeling a little safer. He raised his eyebrows.

"When you start calling me that? You know who I am." I smiled, knowing what he wanted me to say.

"Thank you, papi."

He kissed me on the lips again, and he was gone. He was so smooth and swagged out that I had to figure out a way to slide back in his arms. I needed to get rid of Bizzy so I could get my kids back and move on. Fuck him and his fucked up love.

****

I hadn't heard from Bizzy for a few days, so that made me hope he would just leave me the hell alone now. I felt so good that I wanted to get my hair done so I wouldn't look like a damn fool. Bizzy pulled my damn hair and fucked up my sew-in, so now I had to get myself back together. I chose this new salon called Beauty Queen because a lot of my girls were talking about it. I walked in and had on the biggest pair of sunglasses I could find to hide my face. The place was already packed when I got in there, and I knew I would be waiting a while. *I should have made an appointment,* I thought to myself. I still had Antonio's boy with me, and he was acting like I was the president or some shit. He was kind of annoying.

I went to the desk and the girl was popping gum and looking through her phone. I had to put my face down she could see she had somebody waiting for her ass.

"Can I help you?"

I rolled my eyes up. "Yeah; I wanted to get a sew in; y'all got anybody available now?" I looked at all the filled chairs and saw one that was empty.

"Let me check." I thought she was about to be professional, but this bitch turned around and screamed at the stylist.

"Anybody ready to do her hair?" *This bitch.*

"I'm good over here."

I looked up and saw a dark-skinned chick come from the back. I couldn't help but think she looked just like Kelley Rowland. She waved for me to come to her.

"Hey, what you need done?"

"I need a new weave chile; this shit is all fucked up."

She laughed and directed me to sit in her chair.

"I'm Lashay, by the way. I'm kind of new; that's why I don't have any clients yet. I won't set you up though, I promise."

I smiled at her, and she went to cut my tracks out. We talked for a minute and we clicked right away. She told me about her boyfriend, and how some bitch snuck in and stole him from her.

"Girl, you must not be familiar with the phrase if you surprised by that shit," I said, looking at her through the mirror.

"What phrase?" she said, stopping to look at me.

"BANANAS! Bitches ain't nothing and niggas ain't shit."

The whole shop erupted in laughter.

"I gotta use that one. But yeah; he up and married the bitch too. I ain't trippin' though. I'm coming back strong, believe that." She had this deranged look on her face for a minute, but she caught herself. I hated to be the bitch that got her nigga.

After she did my hair, I made a vow to only come to her. She laid my shit out, and she told me to spread the word. Before I left, I noticed a picture sitting on the desk and it looked like Bella's husband Domo. It couldn't be though; this dude had dreads and shit. He looked like a young nigga too; I wasn't close enough to see his face clearly for real, so I just brushed it off. She gave me her number, and said she wanted to hook up. That was cool; after losing Bella, I needed a friend to chill with.

Later that night, she called me and I was surprised to hear from her so fast. She wanted to hang out and I told her that was cool. She came in acting like we were best friends forever. We talked and smoked, and she was actually cool as shit; she started asking me about myself, and we did the whole Facebook friends thing. She knew quite a few people that I did; she stopped looking in her phone and turned it to me.

"How do you know them?" It was Bella and Domo; that was Bella's profile picture.

"That's my best friend and her husband. Why? You know them?" she shook her head no.

"Nah; the guy just looks real familiar, that's all." She started getting her stuff ready. She seemed to be upset, to be honest, but I didn't push it.

"Aight girl, just hit me tomorrow and maybe we can hang again," I said as she shuffled to the door.

"Yeah; I'd like that, Peaches." She left, and I had an eerie feeling about her all of a sudden. I went back on her Facebook page, and she seemed normal enough. I still just had this feeling that something wasn't right with her.

Chapter 13

Bella

I sat impatiently, waiting for the tech to come get me with a wheelchair. I had been here for four days, and I was ready to go the hell home. Domo was on his phone clicking away, and I wanted to be nosey so I asked him who he was talking to.

"Nobody important, how you feeling?" he tried to skip the subject, but I wouldn't let up.

"If it's nobody important, then why can't you tell me?" he clicked the sleep button on his phone and went to play with the baby.

"So, you just going to ignore me? See, that's why I always think you on bullshit with this secretive stuff."

He smacked his teeth. "Damn man, it's a client, ok? Since when I gotta explain my business to you?"

I knew he was lying. I got up and grabbed his phone from his hand. He was holding DJ., so he couldn't stop me. I put in his passcode, which he didn't think I had, and I went to his last text. The number wasn't saved.

"Bella, give me my fucking phone; you boutta get your issue in a minute." I ignored him and started to read the text.

So you let another chick slide in my place huh? I know you still want me; I'm clean now and we can be together. I love you baby.

Before I could read any more, Domo snatched the phone

from my hands.

"WHO THE FUCK IS THAT BITCH?" I screamed to the top of my lungs. DJ. started crying; I guess I scared him.

"You scaring him. We can talk about this shit later." I knocked over the table, grabbed my duffle bag, and picked up DJ.'s car seat.

"No, fuck you Domo. I'm not going to keep going through this shit with you. The bitch can have you; I mean, I just had our first baby and you texting some bitch in my face? I hate your ass. Fuck that wheelchair, I'm gone." I started walking out when the tech came in and saw the room all messed up from my flipping the table and knocking everything off.

"Sit your ass down and let him take you out." Domo said; I turned to the tech, who was a young cute black boy.

"You can take me wherever you want, baby." He looked scared as shit. He didn't know what to say or do.

"Keep playing with me, Bella. You gonna get this nigga killed fucking with me," Domo said, taking DJ.'s car seat out of my hand. The poor tech ran and left the wheelchair.

"Oh, it don't feel good? How the fuck you think I feel when we gotta keep graving bitches cuz you can't keep your dick in your pants?" I may have said too much, because he had the devil in his eyes.

"You really talking good shit, huh? We gonna see when we get home."

"Ain't no home, it's just me and you playing house apparently. How you let that bitch play with me like that? She clean so y'all can be together now?"

He pulled out his phone and handed it to me.

"Read the rest since you ain't got no faith in a nigga."

I opened the phone and went back to the text. I went back to the last one I read and saw his response.

Nah, you good and she ain't slide in, she took over my ass; I put a ring on my queen and she is more than you ever tried to be to me. I only gave you my number so you can stop harassing my family, but now I see it was a mist12ake. Leave me the fuck alone and don't bother to re-

spond to this; I already spammed your ass.

I looked at him, and he had this look on his face that said *yeah now what.* I felt like a complete jackass once again.

"I'm so sorry. I just...I mean..." I was fumbling over my words because what the hell could I say? He kissed my forehead and I sat down in the chair.

"It's all good. You go hard for your nigga, but you need to pipe the fuck down." I was going to drive myself crazy if I wasn't already there. I guess he meant what he said about not giving my dick away no more. I just had to trust that; it wasn't shit else I could do.

When we got home, I stood in the nursery for almost an hour just watching my baby sleep. He looked so cute, and his room gave me a warm feeling inside; I couldn't believe I was a mommy now. I felt hands wrap around my waist, and he came down and kissed my neck. I loved when he did that. it gave me tingles all over, and his smell was even better. Damn, I loved this nigga.

"You all calmed down now?" I turned around and kissed him on those thick sexy ass lips.

"Yeah, I'm calm. You the one made me this way." I squeezed his dick, and he gave me a smile.

"Yeah; this dick can drive a broad crazy." I pushed his shoulder.

"Well, I better be the only crazy bitch out here. You see I don't play."

"Oh, I meant to tell you. Lando woke up and he said he just remember fucking Lex and somebody shot him. He didn't see who." That was a relief; I didn't want to be the cause of any problems between them.

"Thank God. I'm going to send him some flowers or something." Domo started laughing, but I was confused as to why.

"Babe; that nigga is a straight killa; he don't want no damn flowers. Get him a bottle and some Gas." I guess that made sense; I couldn't see him sniffing no damn roses anyway.

"So whats the plan for tonight? Let's order some food and

watch TV." He grabbed the video monitor receiver for the baby's room and closed the door.

"That sound aight; but don't get any of that Chinese shit; makes my stomach bubble."

I scrunched my face up. "Don't nobody wanna hear about you shitting, boy. Nasty ass." We started going down the steps.

"Oh, it's been plenty of time I went in the bathroom after your ass. Smell like something dead just got flushed." We both started laughing, and then we paused to look at each other.

"That's why I love your ass, girl; you put this smile on my heart like nobody ever could. We like best friends and shit too. That shit is dope," he said, playing in my hair.

"Yeah, it is; I love you too, baby. Now I know I ain't pregnant no more, but can you feed me like a fat pregnant bitch? The hospital food was death on a tray." He pulled out his phone and hit a contact.

"Yeah, this is Dominic Birkdale. I need the works, and it need to be ready in the next two hours; everything on the menu... I know that usually takes days for something like that, but I will buy y'all out for the night and pay y'all triple if you can get it here that fast." He gave whoever he was talking to the address and hung up.

"Who was that?"

"Your food girl, what else?"

I rolled my eyes. "What kind of food, simple?"

He walked over to the couch and flopped down with the remote in hand. "I guess you just gonna have to see, won't you?"

I got excited, and didn't know what for. We watched the ratchetness of Love and Hip Hop, and Domo was into it. I never came across a nigga who wanted to watch this bullshit. He said he liked how they tried to make it real but it was fake as fuck. He had a point. I watched the baby monitor and saw the DJ. was still passed out sleep. The doorbell finally rang, and just on time. A bitch was about to disappear in here. I went to get the door, and when I opened it I was so shocked that I couldn't do shit but stand back as the caterers from Friday's brought the food in. I could smell all the different dishes, and I couldn't help but salivate.

"Boy, you...."

"Too much, I know. Now let them set up and we can get our feast on." Domo said slapping my butt.

He was truly unstoppable. He used Friday's to cater events and meetings he had with clients. I knew when they heard triple, they put everybody the fuck out and started working. I recognized the manager because he always personally ensured the catering.

"David, once again you always come through. Charge my expense account, and here's something for you and your workers," Domo said, handing him a few stacks of money. David's eyes lit up with excitement.

"Thank you, Mr. Birkdale; thank you so much."

When we got into the dining room, the table was filled with food. I saw my favorite, the Cajun shrimp and chicken pasta. I went straight in. Satia walked in and her eyes bugged out.

"Wow, are you pregnant again already?" We laughed.

"Nope, but sit down and eat, take a break."

She gladly pulled up a chair and feasted with us. I had the best man in the world, and couldn't nobody tell me he wasn't.

****

I woke up with a smile on my face because Domo was sitting on the bed feeding DJ., and he looked so happy; he was smiling and kissing him on his little face, and DJ. was just staring up at him with those beautiful big eyes. I rubbed my hand across his back and he turned to me and blew a kiss at me.

"Good morning, sleeping beauty."

"Good morning. Look at my men." I got up to go use the bathroom; I hated talking to him with morning breath. I brushed my teeth and went back to give him a kiss. I cuddled up next to him and enjoyed the family moment.

"I need to run, mami; I got some shit to do. I know this is last minute, but I gotta take a flight to Cuba to check on some shit. That nigga Mario ain't supplying no more, so I gotta press out my Cuban connect because I need more weight than I can get off these local ass niggas." I felt the lump form in my throat.

"We can't go with you? I mean, when are you going?" I felt like I was on the verge of tears. I think it was because I didn't know what he would be doing, and who he would be doing it with. I wanted to trust him because I was wrong about him cheating the last two time I thought I caught him.

"Baby, it's good, don't worry about me. I promise, my dick is safely tucked in my pants. DJ. too young to be traveling anyway. He only a few days old, girl."

"I know, but—"

"It's not going to be long since I'm not bringing shit back, only a few days." I slammed my hand on the bed like a brat. I got up to grab my phone so I could pretend to be doing something so he wouldn't see me about to cry.

"Can you just trust your nigga?"

"I guess; but we tried that, remember? When I was here worried sick and pregnant and you was giving the dick to that French thot." I cut my eyes at him.

"I already apologized a hundred times, shawty; damn. I thought since I been keeping my nose clean, I could get some type of credit. I ain't even sniffing a bitch's way." I rolled my eyes and kept looking through my phone for nothing in particular.

"Aight; we'll see." I threw my phone on the bed and got up; I grabbed DJ. from him and started to burp him.

"I gotta get ready to roll. Won't you try to get some rest so you can work on how you want the spa."

I missed my spa King of Queens, and I had to get my assistant manager to run it until I could get back. I made plans to open a daycare on the property so I could take DJ. with me too. I had to start hiring, so I posted on Indeed and CareerBuilder. I got so many responses in such a short time that I was overloaded just looking at them. Domo told me he would have his architects on it right away, and for me to just worry about healing and making sure DJ. was healthy. He even hired a nanny, but I told him I wasn't on that type of shit and I wasn't some rich bitch who needed others to raise my kid. Satia was helpful, and she was treating DJ. like he was her blood. I loved her so much; she was like another mom to me, and it felt good to have that again.

After Domo left, I was scrolling on my Facebook timeline when I saw a friend request pop up. I didn't recognize the name, so I clicked on the pictures and saw what I believed surely had to be a mistake. It was Domo and some bitch on all the pictures in her album. I looked at the name again, and I almost snapped when I thought about the conversation with his sister about his ex. The name was Lashay Birkdale. I went through the pictures again, and I realized they had to be old. He looked young, and he had long dreads. I didn't even know he had dreadlocks. It said that she'd only been on Facebook for two days. This bitch was sad as shit; she made a page and posted all their pictures up. I screen shot it and sent it to Domo, and he called right away.

"What the fuck, this bitch wild as shit, man," he said when he answered.

"I know; that's some crazy shit; why you ain't tell me you had dreadlocks? You looked cute," I told him.

"I don't know; I cut them after me and that bitch stopped fucking with each other."

"Your sister told me some stuff about y'all; why you didn't tell me you lost a baby?" He was silent. "Hello?" I said into the phone.

"Because it ain't nothing to say. Her ass talk too fucking much. Don't worry about that shit though. What Jr. doing?" He was acting like it was some deep ass secret he couldn't tell me. I pretty much knew, but I wanted to see what he had to say.

"He sleep now; he doesn't really stay up long." I looked at DJ. through the monitor.

"Oh aight. I should be home in a few, aight? Love you."

"Love you too," and we hung up.

This bitch seemed like she was going to be a problem though. Obviously, the trick was delusional as fuck. She didn't want to try to come between me and him; we went hard for each other, and her ass would be another example.

I waited up for Domo, and he finally brought his ass in the

house. I felt a bad vibe as soon as he came in the bedroom.

"What's wrong, boo?" I asked as he sat on the bed and took his shoes off.

"I ran into some shit with Lando's pops earlier. He showed up at the club and said somebody told him that they knew I had something to do with Lando getting popped; I don't know a dumb mufucka who would speak against me. He made his threats and shit, and rolled out. This nigga thinks I tried to have Lando assassinated or some dumb shit."

"I fucked up bad, huh?" I asked, feeling like it was all my fault. I felt real fucked up knowing I got my nigga in some bullshit because of me. I went and started rubbing his shoulders, and he leaned his head back to enjoy the massage. My phone started ringing, and I saw that it was Peaches calling. I ignored it because I still wasn't on good terms with her ass. She called back and I ended the call again.

"You don't fuck with your home girl no more? I noticed she don't be around." I still hadn't told him about what happened at the house that day.

"Nah, we had a little beef and I don't want to be bothered." He picked up the phone when it rang again. I ended the call again; apparently, she didn't get the hint.

"Well, she gonna need a shoulder to cry on after tonight. I'm sending some niggas over there to get Bizzy. That nigga made a bold ass move and thought I wouldn't retaliate. He held my money, then started talking shit to niggas. I should have already got his ass after you told me he called you and shit." I shook my head because there wasn't a *give a fuck* in my body for that nigga. He had the shit coming. Domo's phone started ringing, but he looked at it and put it back down.

"Who you ducking?" I asked, curious as to who he was ignoring.

"That's a blocked number; I think it's Lashay dumb ass." I grabbed the phone and answered. Domo didn't even try to stop me.

"Hello?" the caller didn't speak. "Who the fuck is this; my

husband don't answer blocked calls, so I'm handling his light work."

I heard somebody smack their lips. "Bitch bye," and she hung up.

"You need to tell that bitch wassup; I ain't gonna let her keep playing with me like that."

He shook his head and laid back on the bed. "Don't concern yourself with her; she wished she could be you right now."

I knew she did, but that still didn't make me feel any better that the bitch wouldn't take the hint. I mean, look what happened with that bitch Ja' Tori. She ate my pussy, then tried to kill a bitch. I didn't know what the fuck was up with the bitches he chose, but they seemed a little off.

"I know she do, but you know I will pop the bitch if she don't watch herself."

"Aaaw shit. Lil' Griselda talking that shit again." he tickled my side, and I started laughing.

"Well, you made me this way." I kissed him on the lips and wished I could get some. I had a whole four and a half weeks left before we could fuck.

I wasn't playing though; I was tired of mufuckas thinking they could just disrespect me and think it's cool; that's one thing Domo did teach me. Never take shit from nobody, and never let anybody disrespect me. I was living by that shit now, whether it was him or anybody else. I wasn't having it.

Over the next few days, I enjoyed being a mother; he couldn't do much, but his little face had me lit up every time I looked at him. I was doing a lot of online shopping and burning my debit cards up on him. I bought shit he didn't even need, but I wanted him to have it. I was starting to get stir crazy sitting around, so I told Domo we needed to get out. I was overjoyed when he agreed. We went to dinner at The Cosmo, and I felt so relieved to just have this fresh air.

"How's your food, mami?" I was biting into a huge piece of steak, and he laughed when I tried to answer with my mouth full. "I guess it's no need to ask."

"Shut up. You get on my nerves," I smiled at him. I had this warm feeling in me that nobody could cool off. I was still in love with him, even after all we been through. I didn't know what it was, but I was attached to him in the worst way. When he touched me, the electricity between us was undeniable. You could call me a dumb bitch all day, but you don't know how this man made me feel inside. Even after he fucked around on me, there was something that just kept pulling me to him. I knew it was real love; he was mine, and I was his.

"What you wanna do when we leave?" he asked, sipping his soda.

"I don't know; let's go to the mall." He shook his head.

"You had about two hundred packages delivered this week; what else could you need?"

The couple next to us laughed. The woman looked at me. "That's right girl; shop until you drop. He talk shit to me all the time too," she said, pointing at her man. Domo and the guy looked at each other and shrugged their shoulders, and we shared a laugh.

I had to pee, so I got up and went to the bathroom. I stared in the mirror and saw the change in my face from the small amount of weight I gained during my pregnancy. I patted my stomach that had a small bulge. I was going to be in overtime with the crunches so I could get back to flat. I washed my hands and headed out the door.

I stopped in my tracks when I saw one of the females that used to come to the office to fuck Domo. She was touching my baby and smiling all in Domo's face; I almost flew with how fast I got over there after I saw her give Domo a love-tap on the shoulder. The couple that was just talking to us looked like they were waiting to make a World Star video. I went to the table and stood there like she should have already known to walk away.

"Hey, there you are. You remember Chelsea?" These bitches always seemed to pop up when we were eating and shit. I looked her up and down.

"Don't touch my son; he's a newborn, and I don't know where your hands been." She looked offended and raised her eyebrows.

"I can tell you where they used to be," she said, winking at Domo.

"You right. USED TO BE!" I said, raising my voice. She turned to Domo.

"When you done playing house with this girl, come see a real woman."

I jumped up, and Domo jumped up with me. "Chelsea; stop playing with my wife, bitch—" but she cut him off.

"Hold up, you married this bitch? Wasn't she working for you or something? Thirsty ass bitches always looking for their come up, and I see she trapped you with this baby too," she said kicking DJ.'s stroller. I went to swing, but before I could Domo back-handed the shit outta her. She flew into the couple who was sitting at the table next to us. I was shocked, but I couldn't say she didn't have it coming. I had to pull him away because he was going for her ass.

"Fuck you, nigga. You put your hands on the wrong bitch," she said, backing away embarrassed. The whole restaurant was staring at us.

"Nah, you the right one. You pushed my son, bitch; you got life fucked up," he said, breaking free of me and running toward her.

She hauled ass out the door and he stopped and turned around, looking at all the people who was watching. He came back over and threw a bunch of hundreds on the table, and pushed DJ. out the door. I was right on their tails. I never condoned a man hitting a woman, but that bitch crossed the line bringing our son into the argument and then kicking his stroller. She campaigned for that slap and got elected. Domo opened the door for me and we got in the car. He started the car, but sat back.

"I'm sorry, baby. That bitch just got me hype off that dumb shit."

I looked at him wondering what he was apologizing for. "What you sorry about?"

He looked at me. "For hitting a woman. I try to be a good

man, and to me a man that hits a woman ain't a man. Hitting a bitch is different though." He said in all seriousness.

I shook my head at his silly ass comment. "You're still a man, baby; that bitch had it coming. She kicked our son's stroller. I would have been if mad if you didn't do that shit." He smiled at me, then came toward me and kissed me. He looked back at DJ..

"You ever do what daddy just did, I'ma kick your little ass. Never hit a woman, son."

DJ. was just looking at him, because of course he was a new-born and had no idea what he was talking about. We ended up going to mall and enjoyed the rest of our day.

Domo

I had my assistant making plans for a birthday/baby shower for Bella; she didn't get to have one since she went into labor early, and she didn't have a birthday party since she set it off like Queen Latifah. I was pulling out all the stops; she was going to feel like the queen she was. I made sure to get all of her favorite seafood and pasta for the buffet. She loved cheesecake, so I got twenty different flavors straight from the Cheesecake Factory. I couldn't wait to see the look on her face. I got her a new whip too, and that would be the icing on the cake. It was a 2016 Bentley and I knew once she saw that shit, she would be hopping around like a kid on Christmas day. She was about to be sitting pretty as shit, and I would gladly take the passenger side so she could have her shine. She deserved it.

I left the office heading home to grab some shit for my trip. I couldn't shake the feeling that I was being watched; I knew it was Mario and his peoples. I didn't want shit to happen to Bella and DJ., so I enhanced the security system at the house and even put a twenty-four-hour watch on it. Bella didn't know that though. I didn't want her to worry about shit; I hated to leave and go out the country, but I needed to lock in my plug and let him know I was giving him all my business from now on. He only spoke in person, so that's why I had to take flight.

I called my father to let him know I was about to go holla at them. Even though my pops sat back, he was still very much a part of the game; I just did most of the work. He'd been pressing me out to find out who was talking to Mario in my camp; I felt like it couldn't have been anybody I rolled with, but he insisted that I shook some bushes to see what fell out.

After kissing my beautiful wife and my son, I made my way to the airport to head to Cuba. I sat and waited for the jet to pull up to the gate. I watched all the woman give me the *fuck me daddy* eyes, and I just looked down. I refused to slide my dick in anybody but Bella from now on. I was curving bitches, and it was getting easier and easier to do. I didn't want to tell Bella, but I already knew everything that happened at Peaches and Bizzy's house. I was going to let her tell me, and when she didn't I just figured she wanted to keep me out of it. Antonio already told me everything; Bella told him everything and he told me, just to give me a heads up. That's why I sent my niggas over to Bizzy's spot so soon. They said the nigga wasn't there when they pulled up, so I would have to catch him another day. Peaches, on the other hand, seemed a little disloyal for fucking Bella over like she did. I wanted to fuck her ass up too, but I thought that Bella might want the honor when she felt it was time.

When the jet finally arrived at the gate, I saw my crew pass me and each person spoke. The flight attendant Lacey stopped and gave me a once-over. I hired her not too long ago because the other one I had was pregnant—and no, not by me. I knew what y'all was thinking. I could tell this broad was checking for a nigga hard, and I paid her ass no attention. I boarded and went and sat down, then tried to connect my seat belt; I didn't know what the hell the problem was, but it wasn't snapping in. I looked up just as Lacey tried her best to seductively walk up to me. She leaned in, traced my waist with her hands, and buckled it for me. She looked up and smiled; she had to be about an inch away from my face.

"You're all set, Mr. Birkdale. Is there anything else I can do for you?" I knew what she meant by that and I waved her off.

"Nah, you good. Thanks."

She looked disappointed as she walked to the front and sat in her seat. Damn, she was bad as shit, but fuck that; Bella was badder, and I refused to let my dick get me into any more shit. We took off, and I started getting irritated at the way shawty kept staring at me and shit. Once the seatbelt sign went off, I went into the cabin and sat on the bed. I had a cordless phone by the bed, so I called my baby to see what she was up to.

"Hey mami, you know I miss you already."

I heard her giggle. "You know I'm still mad at you for not taking us."

I smiled at her little spoiled ass. "Don't make me turn this plane around and tell you who daddy is again." I knew she was smiling.

"Well since I'm still bleeding, you can't show me that."

"Yeah, well that butt ain't bleeding," I said, playing with my belt buckle.

"You so nasty, nigga; I miss you already. Oh, I forgot to tell you. You friend stopped by, I told him you weren't here and he left a box for you. He said you been asking for whatever was in there."

Friend? Don't nobody come to my fucking house without me being there. Niggas knew that shit was a no-no.

"Who you talking about? I don't have no friends who randomly show up to my shit."

"Some dude named Paco. I didn't let him in though."

I sat up and opened the door to the cabin. I ran straight up to the front and banged on the door. "Baby, did you open the box? Get DJ. and get the fuck out of there now!" Where the fuck was Goo? That nigga was supposed to be watching my house.

"What's wrong? I didn't open it."

"GET DJ. THE FUCK OUT OF THERE NOW!" The co-pilot opened the door. "Turn this muthafucka around."

"Sir. We're already—"

"Nigga, turn this muthafucka around!" I saw the pilot hit the seatbelt sign, and I went back to sit down. This nigga wanted to play games, huh? Paco was Mario's henchman; he sent that nigga over there with my baby and my wife. I was in a full rage, and I was ready to murder that nigga.

"Baby, you left yet?" I could hear her breathing heavy like she was running.

"Yeah, we're in the car. Baby, what's wrong?"

I heard a loud boom, and then the phone when dead.

"BELLA! BELLA!"

I threw the cordless phone on the floor and put my face in my hands. I got up and grabbed the phone, and tried calling her back. She didn't answer; it just kept ringing and going to voice-mail, so I got my cell phone to get Antonio's number. I called from the air phone and he picked up.

"Get over to our house; I think something happened to Bella and DJ.. I need you to go see about them," I said in a panicked tone.

"WHAT! I'm on the way. Are you headed home?"

"Yeah; I was on the way out of town, and she called saying one of Mario's niggas dropped off a package; it sounded like some shit blew up. Hit my cell when you get there!" I hollered into the phone.

"Aight, calm down; I will call you when I get there." He hung up, and I started thinking the worst; we couldn't be far because we were only in the air for about an hour.

"We're about to land, Mr. Birkdale."

I was so anxious to get off the jet that my leg was shaking. As soon as we got to the gate, I was trying to get out the door. Lacey came over and unlocked it; she tried to let her hand slide over my dick on purpose, and I mean mugged the bitch.

"Bitch, your thirsty ass is fired," I said, pretty much jogging down the terminal. My phone started ringing, and it was Antonio.

"Domo, they're fine. Your maid got caught in the blast, and she is on the way to the hospital in critical condition."

Thank God; I hoped that Satia was going to be ok. This nigga just started a fucking war and if I had to go, I was taking a lot of them muthafuckas down with me.

I ran the whole way to the garage and jumped in my whip. I made it to our block in record time. There were ambulances and firefighters everywhere. I saw my home burning to the ground, and I couldn't do shit about it. I started looking for Bella and DJ., but I couldn't pick them out with so many people crowding the street. I called Antonio to see where they were.

"I'm at the house; where are you?"

"We're sitting in the ambulance at the end of the block."

I saw it sitting at the corner and started running to it. I saw Bella sitting in the back; she looked so scared that I started feeling bad for even leaving her. I should have been there.

"Baby, oh my God. I'm so sorry." I hugged her and kissed all over her face. I looked at her and DJ., and they didn't have a scratch on them.

"We could have died, baby; what if you didn't call? Who would do something like this?" I shook my head because I knew exactly who was about to die behind this shit. Antonio pulled me to the side.

"Do I need to be scared of my daughter being with you? This is unacceptable in my eyes." I looked at this nigga sideways. I had respect for him, but the last thing he needed to do was question how far I would go to protect my wife and son.

"I didn't send a bomb to my own fucking house. Somebody did this shit, and I know who; you don't have to worry about shit. I got Bella."

I turned my back to him and went back to Bella and my baby boy. I wouldn't know what to do if I lost them. I knew I had to go see Lando; I wanted to see what he knew about this shit. He was out of the hospital, so I knew he was home; I called him and told him I would be by to see him tonight. He said that was cool, and he didn't sound alarmed or anything; I knew he didn't know shit, but a nigga always had to cover his bases.

After the show was over, the neighbors went back inside and the block started to clear. The detectives asked if I knew who would want to harm my family, and of course I said no. I'm a street justice nigga, and I didn't need the police to help me lay these mufuckas down. I texted all my muscle because I was going to need them. Before we left, we got some news that fucked me up even more. Satia died shortly after she was taken to the hospital. That shit broke a nigga's heart because she had been working for me since I had my first apartment. I didn't even know how to break the shit to her family.

I almost forgot about Goo's ass; I hadn't seen him since I pulled up. I searched the block for him, and his car was nowhere to be found. I called his phone, but it went straight to voicemail. I had a feeling that nigga wasn't gone of his own free will; there was no way that nigga would roll out and disrespect my orders. I called a meeting for all my muscle at my crib on the beach for the morning. I needed to find the snake in my grass; somebody was answering for this shit.

****

I couldn't get any sleep the whole night; I was supposed to meet up with Lando last night, but I didn't want to leave Bella and DJ. alone. Bella was shaken up, and I couldn't blame her. Antonio offered to watch over them, but there was something about his demeanor I didn't trust all of a sudden. It was like he was too calm about this shit, and it just didn't sit right and since I didn't know why, I just didn't trust him anymore. Bella was stirring around and she turned over toward me; she opened her pretty ass eyes and smiled at me.

"Good morning, Domo; your eyes are bloodshot red. Did you sleep?" she asked, sitting up on her elbow.

"Nah, not really. I wanted to make sure niggas wasn't coming back."

She looked at the little bassinet we picked up last night, and DJ. was sound asleep. We had to buy diapers, wipes, and everything we lost for him. I started getting mad all over again.

"Did you tell anybody about what happened with Lando?" She looked down on the bed, and I knew she did.

"I just talked to my father about it. That's it." She looked like she was on the verge of tears, so I softened my face so she wouldn't be scared.

"Oh really? Well, I'm asking because somebody told Mario that I knew something about what happened to his kid. I didn't want to scare you, so I didn't tell you Lando was Mario's son."

"Is he coming to get me? Is that why this happened?"

"Baby, you know I don't give a fuck what you did; ain't nobody touching you, mami. I got you."

I kissed her and got up to get ready. I knew I had a feeling, and I could bet you a hundred fucking dollars that he went to Mario. I couldn't jump the gun because I could be wrong. I mean, Drake was there too, but I ain't have that gut instinct that said he was the rat. It was Antonio; it's always been his ass. She must have known what I was thinking.

"You can't think my father did this. Papa would never put me in danger; I mean, what would be the damn reason?" That I didn't know.

"I ain't saying nothing; I'm just wondering, you know." I played it off because I didn't want her to tell him; I'd rather catch him off guard to gauge his reaction.

"I feel you. What time you coming home?" she asked, getting up and walking to her dresser. I had a lot of shit to do, so I couldn't even give her a real timeframe.

"I don't know yet; I got somebody on the door and somebody downstairs. Call me if anything seems funny, aight?" I leaned in and kissed her on those plump pink lips.

"Ok, just please hurry back. I don't want to be alone."

I nodded my head and went to get in the shower. I hit Drake and told him to make sure everybody was ready to meet up. As soon as I got in the shower, my phone alerted me that I had a text. I leaned out to grab my phone, and when I opened the message I got irritated and threw it back on the counter. Lashay must have changed her number again so she could get through on my phone since I blocked her ass. It was a picture of her pussy. I was going to make sure to change my number today.

After I got myself together, I told Bella I loved her and that I would be back as soon as I could. I started my car and turned on the radio. I nodded my head to Future's *Fuck up some comma's.* My assistant called me to confirm some things about Bella's party. I told her to do as she felt; I also told her I would send her some addresses so she could send my condolences to Satia's family. I was going to make a trust for her grandkids; I knew how much she loved them, so I wanted to make sure they would be ok.

I pulled up to the meeting, and I made my way to the door.

Before I touched the knob, it swung open; Drake was standing to the side for me to walk in.

"What up, Domo?" They all slapped hands with me, and I stood in the middle as they surrounded me.

"I know y'all heard about what happened at my house. We coming back hard! The nigga Mario crossed the line, and we need to show these mufuckas that the Birkdale niggas ain't to be fucked with!"

They all dapped each other up and turned their attention back to me. Juice was one of my crazier niggas. He didn't give a fuck what the problem was; he was laying everything down without question. He stepped forward to speak.

"What Lando think about us gunning for his pops?" I would have to talk to him on my own.

"Nothing, because I didn't have words with him yet. Let me worry about him, aight?" They all nodded in agreement.

"Look, we making this move tonight. We going in and we clearing that bitch out! You feel me? This nigga tried his hand, and he folded. Brook and Mel, I need to holla at y'all niggas. I got y'all on a different move. Aight, Drake gonna hit all y'all with the meeting spot. Be ready to work." They nodded and started to file out. Brook, Mel, and Drake were the only ones left.

"I need y'all to follow Bella's pops around. That nigga up to some shit, but I just don't know what it is. Let me know what y'all come across, aight?"

"You know we on that shit, boss," Brook said as they walked out.

"Why Antonio? He seem pretty straight to me," Drake asked.

"I know a snake nigga; you should know that more than anybody. It's either you or him, and I don't feel like it's you so that leaves his ass. Bella told him what happened, and all of a sudden Mario getting information about that day. I call bullshit." Drake nodded and shrugged his shoulders.

"Well, you know if we gotta put in work on that nigga, Bella might have an issue with it." He was right, but she would never know.

"Y'all get up with that nigga Bizzy yet? This nigga done turned ghost, huh?" I was ready to go to my next move.

"Oh shit; my bad, nigga. That nigga got knocked; I don't know what happened yet, but the boys picked up him the day after Bella had the baby.

"Aight; as soon as that nigga touch down, turn him into a case." Drake nodded and walked out. I was walking to the car when my phone started ringing. It was my mother. I rolled my eyes up and answered.

"Yeah."

"Dominic, I need you to come get me."

She must have been high; she wasn't allowed in any of my cars since the last time I picked her up; she stole my fucking radio when I went to grab her some food from Burger King. She was gone by the time I came back out.

"You know I can't do that. You robbed your own son the last time I tried to help, Ma." She started crying.

"Baby, your momma's sick. I can't barely do nothing but breathe. I got bone cancer, son." I closed my eyes as those words sunk in.

"What you need, Ma?"

"I just need a place to sleep; I can't take care of myself no more."

"Aight. I can put you in a hotel, is that cool?"

"I can't stay with you? You got that little bitch who shot me now, so I guess not." All my compassion started to wither.

"Ma, I promise you as your son that if you ever disrespect my wife again, that cancer won't beat me to your grave. She was protecting my sister who you had tied up in the fucking nasty ass hole you called a home. You don't even deserve my help, but since you birthed me I'm going to help you out."

I know I sounded cruel, but she lost my respect a long time ago. I found out she was tricking and got pregnant with my little sister Marion. I thought the pregnancy would at least help her get off the shit, but as soon as she pushed Marion out she left her at the hospital to get high. I had to find her and bring her back before they sent Marion to child services. I found her in the crack house and dragged her out of there, and back to the hospital. I told them she left to get her medicine. They didn't think much of it until she went into a rage because she wanted to get high. They called the police, and I grabbed my sister and left before they came. They locked my mother up because she beat up one of the nurses and tried to stab the another with a pen; I had to raise my little sister for the first years of her life.

"Thank you, Dominic; you know I love you, right?"

"Yeah, I know Ma. Where you at?" I asked, finally starting my car. I was sweating hard as shit, and I needed that air conditioning to come through for a nigga.

"I'm at aunt Boo Boo's house." I didn't want to go there, by any means. All my family cared about was how much money I could loan them, and what I could do for their past due bills and shit.

"Be ready when I get there."

I hung up and made the drive to my aunt's house. When I pulled up, there was niggas everywhere; she kept a full house, and I had no idea who these mufuckas was. My mother was sitting on the porch smoking a cigarette. I blew my horn, and all the fuck niggas started staring. She got up and limped over to the car.

"Your Aunt Boo Boo wants to say hi," she said, leaning into my window.

"I don't give a fuck what she want; let's go. I got moves." She opened the door and got inside.

"Damn, when the last time you took a bath?"

She smiled and most of her teeth were missing. "I don't know boy; you know I ain't have no water in months."

I gritted my teeth and drove off. She didn't have to be this way. She had a good life at first and she threw it away. I wanted to drop her off as soon as possible. She had my car smelling like the back of an ear that ain't been washed, and I didn't want it to linger.

"Come on. I promise you, Ma; don't fuck this up or you will never get another helping hand from me." She started getting out, and out of the little bit of respect I still had for her, I told her to hold up so I could open the door.

"You always been such a gentleman, baby. I'm glad I raised you right."

I helped her out and finally got the full extent of how weak she was. She was shaking as she walked. She coughed in a napkin she had been holding, and there was blood on it.

"Nah, you know what? Let me take you to the hospital."

I helped her back in and she didn't fight me on it. I had to run, so I called my sister to come be with her. She loved my mother more than anything in the world; no matter what my mother did, she always had her back. I told her I was taking her to Sanai, and she told me she would be there as soon as she could. When we got there, I explained everything to the receptionist and she told me we had to wait because there wasn't an emergency at the moment.

"Hey Ma, hey big bro," Charlene said, coming in with that bum ass nigga; his face was still fucked up from when I put that steel to his bitch ass.

"Look after Ma for me. I got shit to do; let me know what they say."

She nodded her head and sat down next to my mother. I shook my head at this nigga who was scared to even look my way. I left the hospital and made my way to the next spot. I thought I was tripping when I saw this bitch drive past me at the intersection, but I wasn't. I followed her all the way to a salon called Beauty Queens. I watched her get out her car, and I quickly went to stop her before she went in.

"Shay!" She quickly turned her head when she heard my voice. She looked good, like she hadn't been using that shit for a while.

"Hey baby, I knew you couldn't stay away." She came in close to me, and I pushed her back.

"You sent my wife a friend request? Then she tell me you posting up our old ass pictures to make her mad and shit."

She smacked her teeth. "Nigga please; you only with her

because I left. You know what else? I think you're real fucked up for giving that baby our son's name," she said, acting like she was about to cry.

"Bitch, you still high? We were having a girl. You know what? Fuck all this, and do me a favor. Stop playing games; you know what can happen when I get mad. So stop fucking with me and my wife. Last time I'm going to say it."

She looked in the shop, and I saw the bitches' faces pressed on the glass. These hoes ain't have shit else to do. I was walking to my car, and I heard the footsteps behind me.

"Baby, I know I did some shit I ain't proud of, but you can give me another chance to show you I'm different." I stopped and looked to the sky.

"You ain't got shit to show me, Shay. My queen makes me happy, and she don't need to be stressing over some shit that's dead." I opened my door and got in.

"I thought I was your queen."

I laughed and started my car. "You dethroned yourself when you was shooting that shit and fucking anything with a dick attached to it. You killed our baby…man, I ain't got time for this shit. Cut the bullshit, Shay."

"What about you, Domo? Huh? You sooooo perfect. Nothing is ever wrong with Dominic fucking Birkdale. I bet you didn't tell her, did you? Yeah nigga, I remember everything. That's why I was shocked to see you with her." I grabbed her around the throat and started to squeeze.

"Ain't shit to tell; if I hear you even thought about running your mouth, I will bury your ass, bitch." I let go and got into the car.

I drove off and watched her stand there holding her throat and coughing. I stopped at the light and when I looked in my rearview, I saw her following me. I was hoping I wouldn't have to murder this bitch in broad daylight, but she turned off and I felt at ease. I texted Lando to tell him I would be there in about an hour. He said that was cool because his new girl was coming through, and he wanted to hit it before I came. My nigga still recovering, and he worried about some pussy.

As I drove, I thought about what Lashay said; I hated to hold this from Bella, but I knew it would break her heart and I couldn't stand to see her hurt again. Ain't no point in bringing up the past. It's best to let sleeping dogs lie. I knew that if she knew about how her mother really died, she wouldn't want anything to do with me.

I made my way to Lando's spot, regardless of what he said. When I pulled up, I stopped and smirked as I watch this stupid bitch leave his building and get into her car. She was going to be a problem.

Chapter 14

Bella

"Waaaaaaah waaaaaaaaaaaah!"

I woke from my nap to the sounds of DJ. crying. I got up to grab him when the door flung open, and Domo walked in. It was nighttime and the room was dark, so I couldn't really see anything. I heard his panting, and I jumped up to turn the light on. He was completely covered in blood. DJ. was still crying, so I went and picked him up. I turned my attention back to Domo, who was now in the bathroom taking his clothes off.

"What happened?" He turned the shower on and turned to me.

"I don't really want to talk about it. It's a lot you wouldn't understand." I hit the start button on DJ.'s Baby Brezza so it could make his bottle.

"You need to tell me something. You came in here covered in fucking blood, Domo."

"I went to talk to Lando about some shit. When I got there, I saw Lashay leaving his spot. He told me the bitch approached him while he was getting his prescription from CVS. I'm sure it was a planned move; she trying to start some shit."

"So you killed them? You must still have feelings for the bitch then."

He gave me a cold stare. "I didn't touch them; I told you she was leaving when I got there. I didn't give a fuck who she was fucking. I just needed to talk to my nigga, and he must have known I saw her so he wanted to explain."

"Ok, so whose blood is that?"

"I was getting to that if you stop making assumptions. I left Lando after hearing what I already knew, and I went to meet up with some of my folks tonight after I left the office. When we got to the spot, somebody came by and started spraying at us, and Drake got hit. He was bleeding out, so I tried to stop it; that's why I look like this."

"Is he ok?"

He shook his head no. "He died when we got to the hospital."

Damn; that shit was fucked up. He was a cool dude too. "I'm sorry to hear that, babe. What were you all doing anyway?"

"We had to meet up with somebody; that's all, babe."

He wasn't telling me everything, but I knew he was fucked up so I left it alone. His phone started ringing and he picked it up.

"What's up, man...yeah, this shit fucked up." He waited for the other person to talk. "You sure...aight look, you and Mel go holla at Vibe for me. This shit ain't gonna be as easy as I thought." He hung up.

"What's wrong now?"

"Nothing. Look, I'm taking a break from work for a while. I know you were looking forward to going back to the spa, but it's just not safe out here."

I was so disappointed to hear him say that. I didn't want to be trapped in the house all day. "Uggghhh aight. Did you eat?" I started to feel saddened by the fact Satia wasn't here anymore. I sent her daughter some cards and ordered her some flowers. Domo and I already told them we would be paying for all the funeral expenses. She was such a sweet lady.

"Nah, I'm not really hungry. I just need to get some sleep, mami." He closed the bathroom door.

I fed DJ. his bottle and changed his diaper. He went right back to sleep after that. I knocked on the bathroom door to see if Domo needed anything. I heard the condo's doorbell ring, and I went to answer it. I only met Domo's father twice, but I knew that was him when I looked through the peephole. I opened the door and he walked in without saying anything to me.

"Um…I don't care who you are to Domo. You don't just brush past me and not say shit."

He turned to look at me. "You got a mouth like your mother, you know that?"

I paused when I heard him bring up my mother. I mean, I guess he must have known her because he knew my father. I was still irritated as shit that he just barged in here like that.

"Yeah, whatever. I'm going to tell Domo you're here." I started to feel uncomfortable because he watched me walk to the back. I turned the door knob, and Domo was drying off.

"Your father is here. He basically knocked my ass down coming in."

He smacked his teeth. "Ok, tell him I'm coming. Matter of fact, don't. just wait in here for me, aight?"

Good, I didn't want to be around the creep. He threw on a t-shirt and boxers and stepped out the door, closing it behind him. I was nosey as shit, so I went and cracked the door. I could clearly hear their voices.

"You need to put a muzzle on her ass; she got a smart ass mouth," I could hear his father say. Fuck him.

"Stop talking shit about my wife, Pops. You know I don't play when it comes to her. What you doing here anyway?"

"I heard about your young nigga getting bodied. Seems like a lot of your soldiers falling now."

"Don't worry about it. I got this," Domo said, and from the tone of his voice he was getting upset.

"Yeah, I knew you would say that. I reached out to Mario myself to find out what the fuck was going on."

"What the fuck you do that for? You think I can't handle my business or something?" Domo raised his voice.

"You need to calm the fuck down and remember who you talking to, nigga. He told me somebody let him know that it was your wife who shot his son. Is that true?"

My heart stopped when I heard that. I was getting every

other word after that shit. I calmed down and kept listening.

"He wants her, Domo. How the fuck you gonna handle that shit? Look what he did so far. You think he gonna stop?"

"That nigga ain't touching mine. She ain't do shit. I told you I don't know who the fuck did it. I was going there tonight, but then this bullshit happened and I got sidetracked."

"Well, you need to do something. He won't even hear me out about the shit. You need to make him believe it's a lie, or you can say bye to your wife."

My heart was beating out of my chest.

"I'm going to talk to him again, but it's out of my hands if I can't make him think otherwise."

"Aight, Pops. Holla at you later, man."

I closed the door, went to the bed, and acted like I didn't hear anything. When he came in, he gave me a smile but I guess my face told it all.

"You heard, didn't you?"

I nodded my head yes. "Is that man really going to kill me? Is that what that shit at the house was about?"

He sat on the bed and exhaled deeply. "Yeah, Baby. Somebody told him about what happened, and I been trying to find out who."

I started to cry, and he pulled me to him and wiped my face. "What are we gonna do, Domo?"

He rubbed his hands down my arm. "I would die fighting for you, Bella; I ain't boutta let nobody hurt you or DJ.." He kissed me, and I believed him. I was still scared; he couldn't be everywhere.

****

I hadn't talked to Peaches since the day I had DJ. I was more than surprised when my father showed up at the condo, and had her with him.

"Why you bring this bitch here?" My father looked confused. I guess she didn't tell him what went down.

"C'mon, Bella; let's go talk and let this shit go; you know how much your friendship means to me."

"Bitch, if my friendship meant anything, you wouldn't have

fucked Drew and had a baby with him. If I didn't come to your house, I never would have known, huh?"

My father let her go. "Really? Why you ain't tell me this shit?" My father looked at her for an answer. She looked like a deer caught in headlights.

"It was a mistake! Damn, nobody makes mistakes but me?" Domo came walking out the back with DJ. in his arms.

"What the hell is going on out here? Y'all woke the baby up screaming and shit." Domo said with a scowl on his face.

"I was just waiting for Peaches to explain how she fucked Drew and my godson was their baby." Domo shook his head.

"Well, what you wanna do? You want her the fuck outta here?" Domo said, mean-mugging Peaches. My father gave Domo the side eye.

"I came here to see my grandson. I ain't got time for this girl shit, man."

Peaches had tears in her eyes, and for the sake of my baby I calmed down. "Nah, she here with papa. But after he spend his time with DJ., she can get the fuck out," I said, and walked off into my room. Domo came in shortly after without the baby. I knew my father was in there plotting to spoil him rotten.

"Why you ain't tell me that why y'all fell out." I had my knees under my chin, sitting on the bed and pretending to be watching TV.

"I didn't think it was important."

He stood over me. "Well, it's important enough for you to be screaming on her. I already knew anyway." How this nigga know every fucking thing before I tell him? I shrugged my shoulders.

"I'm saying, you wouldn't be a little fucked up about that shit?" I looked up at him.

"Yeah, but let me ask you something—and please don't get mad. How can you keep forgiving me all those times and you can't forgive her once? She helped you get your spot and some more shit when you left Drew. I think you should go make up with your friend and move past this. People fuck up all the time Bella;

Yeah, I wouldn't fully trust her but she loves you and I can tell she fucked up about the shit. I ain't saying you gotta marry her ass just talk and see how you feel after that." Damn, this nigga just made some type of sense.

"I guess I never thought about it like that. I don't know, though." he stood me up.

"I know it's hard, but people fuck up; let that shit be dead with his ass." I smiled up at him.

"Aight, but I'm telling you. You and her got one more time to fuck Bella Birkdale over."

He raised his eyebrows and smirked. "I ain't tryna get shot, so I been a good boy."

He laughed, and I gave him a kiss. I walked back out to the living room, and Peaches was holding DJ. and smiling at him. I did miss her, but I didn't want to be stupid anymore either. I was going to just let the shit be fifty; she would have to earn my friendship back.

"Peaches." She jumped when I called her name.

"Hey, I was just about to give him back to Antonio." She sounded like she was caught doing something she wasn't supposed to be doing.

"It's ok; you can bring him with you." I saw the hope spread across her face. She got up and followed me into the bedroom.

"You can lay him in his crib," I said.

"Bella, I know I fucked up. You gotta believe me when I say it wasn't planned," she said, not wasting any time.

"I know, but you still broke my heart with that shit, Peaches. Damn!" I yelled, feeling angry again.

"I know, I know. I love you like a sister, Bella. I'm sorry, I really am. I own this shit sis."

"Aight, Peaches; but believe me when I say; don't try me again. I had enough of people thinking they can run over me and I ain't having the shit no fucking more. If I even think you on some underhanded shit than its me and you." I said flaring my nostrils and meaning every word. Aint no more, weak ass Bella.

"I understand; so can we be cool?" She asked with a slight

smile. I still felt some type of way.

"You should be thanking Domo because I was ready to kick your ass and throw you out." She laughed and came in for a hug.

"I got my boo back. I thought I was gonna have to break in a new friend. I been chilling with my stylist lately. She cool as shit, though," she said, running her hands through her weave.

"Damn, she banged that shit," I said, looking over her new hair style.

"Yup, you should get her to do yours."

"Nah, I only get my shit done by the Dominicans; you know that." It got quiet, and we just looked at each other.

"Thank you," she said with tears building in her eyes.

"For what?" I asked, confused.

"For taking me back as a friend. I know a lot of bitches wouldn't have even looked at me twice again," she said, wiping her eyes.

"Well, everybody fucks up. Just don't cross me again, Peaches. I ain't the same Bella," I said seriously. She must have known I meant it because her face was just as serious as mine.

"I got you."

We went on talking, and Domo came in the room. "Damn, I missed the cat fight?" I sucked my teeth.

"Wasn't no cat fight; we good, though."

"Well, that's good to know; but Peaches, if you ever fuck my wife over like that again, you dealing with this nigga. You feel me?" he said, pointing at his chest. She nodded her head.

"I gotta bounce. Oh, Peaches; your old nigga said he was heading out, and if you wanted a ride you need to come on."

I slapped his arm. "Don't call my father old. He still fine, that's how he pulling these young hoes." Peaches had her mouth open.

"Really bitch? Fuck you too." We all laughed, and it felt like old times with her. She kissed my cheek and left out. I followed her to say goodbye to Papa, but he was already gone. Damn; he ain't even say bye. I locked the door after Peaches left and went back into the room.

"Come look at this, Baby. You like it?" I went and sat next to him and looked at his laptop screen.

"WHOOOOAH! Don't tell me that's what you're looking at for us." I started clicking through the pictures of the house that literally sat on the beach. I was falling in love with the pictures alone.

"You know I only get the best, baby. I got a surprise for you next week too. Don't bother to ask me what it is either; you know I love the look on your face when I make your day," he said, closing the laptop and sitting it on the nightstand.

"You do too much for me, baby." He picked me up and laid me on top of him.

"I don't think I do enough. You deserve it all, mami, and I'm going to give it to you." We started kissing, and he slid his hand down my ass. I started throbbing, and this pad I had on made me remember I was still bleeding and couldn't have sex.

"You know we can't."

"I know. I was just closing my eyes and imagining being in this pussy."

I busted out laughing. I couldn't have sex, but I could do something to give him a good nut. I started unbuckling his jeans, and I slightly yanked them down. His dick sprung up like a jack in the box, and I went in head first. I slowly took it down inch by inch, until I gagged. I rubbed the spit up and down it, and bobbed my head on it until I felt the vein popped up.

"Damn baby, you got a nigga ready to bust."

I stopped and looked up. "Nope, you ain't cumming until I say you can." I licked the tip.

"Sssssssss, fuuuuuuuck."

I felt his legs tighten, and I knew I was working that dick. My jaws were hurting something serious, but I kept going. He grabbed the back of my head, and just when I felt like he was about to cum I stopped again.

"Stop playing, Bella."

I giggled and went back on it, and deep-throated as much as I could. He gripped my hair so I would get back up, and he nutted down my throat.

"Damn, I don't even want the pussy no more; just give a nigga that throat." I started laughing and like clockwork, DJ. woke up crying.

"I got him."

Domo got up and fixed himself while I went to the bathroom to brush my teeth and gargle. I heard a vibration and saw that Domo's phone was sitting on the countertop. I gently locked the door so he wouldn't break in on me. I went into his phone and saw he had new text messages; they were from Brook. It was a picture. When I opened it, I got so pissed off. I didn't even care if he knew I went through his phone or not. I yanked the door open and threw it at him.

"Why you got a nigga following Papa?"

He looked at the picture and shook his head. "You know why? You see this house he in front of?" I looked at the picture again.

"Yeah, so?" I said, snapping with much attitude.

"That's Mario's house. I fucking knew it. You said you told him what happened, didn't you? Why the fuck is Mario all of a sudden saying somebody told him everything? Look at this shit, Bella; it's in your face!"

I didn't want to believe my father almost got me killed. There was no way he would do something like that to me.

"No, there has to be another reason. I don't believe that shit."

"Well don't. I gotta run."

I ran behind him. "Where are you going?" I yelled as he grabbed his keys and left.

"Where you think I'm going? Sorry Bella, but your pops a dirty motherfucka."

He left out and slammed the door. I ran to my phone to call my father, but he didn't pick up. I sent him a text and waited for him to answer, but he never did. I called Peaches.

"Peaches, where's Papa?" I said panicking.

"I don't know; he got a text and left. He said it was one of his friends from back in the day." I hung up and started crying. I put DJ. back in his crib and called Domo.

"Bella, ain't shit you can tell me right now. My son almost died because of this nigga."

I started crying. "Domo, please; I can't let you do this."

"So you're against me is what you're saying."

I cried even harder. "No, baby. I'm not against you; you don't even know if the shit is true or not. My father could be trying to help us," I pleaded with him.

"I know you love him, mami; but I just…"

He paused, and I heard sirens and shit in the background.

"What's going on?" I asked in a panicked tone.

"I don't know; there's police and shit on Mario's street. They carrying bodies out from what I can see."

"Oh my God!" I cried. I could hear Domo talking to somebody in the background.

"Who you talking to?" I asked, ready for answers.

"Mel; he said after your father went in; it was guns blazing, and he saw your father run out and jump in the car."

There was a loud banging at the door and it startled me. Domo had a guy sitting out there at all times, so I didn't know who the hell he would let bang on the door like that.

"Somebody banging on the door, Domo. I'm scared." I could hear tires screeching.

"Baby, don't open it; stay on the phone with me." I walked in the living room to look out the peephole. When I saw who it was, I swung the door open. I didn't see Domo's guy.

"Papa. I was so scared." He came in, and I noticed he was holding his stomach.

"Your pops there!" I forgot Domo was on the phone.

"You gotta go, Papa. Domo thinks you told Mario I tried to kill his son."

"No, don't go. Stay." I turned to see a gun pointed at me and my father. I was so shocked I couldn't even move.

"Bella is that—"

He snatched the phone from me and threw it on the ground.

"Y'all stole my life from me. It's payback time."

Domo

When Bella's line went dead, I did the whole dash all the way to the condo; I could have sworn I heard my father's voice before the line went dead. I made it there in record time, and I ran up the stairs up and ran down the hall. Carlos, the nigga that was supposed to be watching the door, was laid out with a blood puddle around him. I pulled out my Glock and cracked the door open. I heard my father talking, and I saw Bella and her pops sitting on the couch. DJ. was screaming his lungs out in the back. What the fuck was this nigga doing?

"You stole my woman and had this little bitch." Antonio looked confused when he said that.

"I ain't steal shit from you, nigga. What the fuck are you talking about? I was loyal to your ass, nigga; and this how you do?" My father let off a shot in the air.

"You knew I was in love with her. She told me you suspected something, but you just didn't know who it was that was fucking your wife."

Bella was crying and sitting on the couch. This was the first time I was hearing this shit. I had a whole different version. When I was younger, I was sitting at the table with Lashay and my pops when he told me that he had a lesson for me. He told me all about how his partner Antonio's wife, Bella's mother, was stealing out of their stash and he chased her down, and she crashed and died.

He told me that's how you deal with disloyal motherfuckas. You take them out. Now I see that was all a lie.

"You fucked my wife, motherfucka?" Antonio lunged at him, but my father hit him in the head with the gun and he fell.

"Yeah, in every hole I could fit in. That bitch told me she wanted to stay with you and your fucking daughter, and she wanted to end shit. I couldn't have that. Now you're back, and your daughter is worse than that hoe. She fucking my son's head up and fucking up our business. I had to get rid of her somehow. So I thought what better way to kill two birds with one stone?" I heard enough.

"It was you?"

He turned and pointed the gun at me, and I had mine pointed at him. He started laughing.

"Yeah; pretty clever, huh? When I first met Bella, I knew exactly who she was; she made me sick to even look at her. Your nigga Drake was so comfortable telling me everything that happened; I knew she would tell daddy everything, and since I knew you would be wondering what happened I just let the chips fall. I sent this fool a text saying meet me and it was about Bella. I gave him Mario's address. I knew you had somebody watching him, so I let the shit play out in movie fashion. I didn't think he would make it out of there though." He kicked Antonio in the stomach.

"You almost killed my son, Pops. And for what? Over some shit that happened almost twenty years ago?"

"Fuck that little bastard. He got this pussy's blood in him, so he ain't shit to me either. Matter of fact, I'm getting tired of his fucking crying." He tried to go to the back, and I shot him one in the leg." Bella was screaming when the blood splattered across her face.

"You would shoot your own father when his back's turned?" he said, raising his gun and before I could shoot, he had a hole in his chest the size of a fist. I turned to where the shot came from, and Bella was holding a pump I kept behind the couch cushion. She was panting heavy, and she dropped the gun and ran to the back to get DJ.."

I helped Antonio up and he sat on the couch. "So you thought I would kill my own child huh?" he said, looking up at me.

"I ain't gonna lie; yeah. I was coming for you."

He laughed and laid back. "I don't blame you. I would have done the same thing. You got my respect, brother." He reached his hand out to shake my hand, and I accepted it.

"You don't have to worry about Mario; when I got the text, I rounded up some of my boys and we headed over there. I knew it was a setup once I got there and the nigga looked at us like we was crazy. I went in there to find your father and they all started shooting. so we shot at them. Everybody in that bitch is gone."

I shook my head. How could I have not seen this shit? I was so focused on Antonio that I didn't think of any other scenarios. Who the fuck would have thought it was my pops though? I watched his lifeless body lay on the floor. I wanted to feel something, but there wasn't shit to feel. I hated to call the police, but I had to. I heard the sirens, and I knew they were coming. I grabbed all the guns I had in the house and threw them down the trash chute.

"Bella, come here!" I yelled in the back.

"You need to leave. Take your father to the hospital, and I will meet y'all there." She was still crying as she walked over my father's body. I quickly ran down to the security office. They were already on the way up by the time I got to the bottom floor.

"I got fifty G's for those tapes from tonight," I told the two young niggas before they even had a chance to say shit. They looked at each other and ran back down, and I followed them. They handed me the DVDs, and I told them to meet me tomorrow and gave them my card with my number on it.

"You good for it, right?" the fat one asked

"Nigga, shut the fuck up and take the card. You already know."

I left out the back and watched all the police file in. I waited about forty-five minutes, and went back upstairs. When I got to the door, the police stopped me. Carlos was still in the same position he was in when I first walked up.

"This is a crime scene, sir; we can't let anybody past this line."

"That's my company's condo. The security called me and told me I needed to get down here." The two security guards who gave me the DVDs were standing there nodding at the officer.

"Yeah, this is his place."

"I'm sorry to tell you this; there's a body lying on the floor of your living room. Do you know how it got here? Also, do you know this man here?"

"How the fuck am I supposed to know? I just pulled up. His name was Carlos; he was a member of my security staff."

The officer put his hand up in an attempt to calm me down. I was playing a mean role right now.

"Would you like to see if you know the man?"

I nodded and walked in the living room; my father was still laying on the floor. He had a sheet over him now. The coroner lifted the sheet back.

"That's my father! Pops!" I screamed, and went back outside of the condo.

"That's your father?" I nodded yes with my hand on the bridge of my nose, like I was distraught. "Did you know he was coming by? I mean, this is strange. There no forced entry. Did he have a key?" he asked.

"Yes; there was a spare over the door." I had already placed it in his pocket before I left.

"Well, we're going to need to follow up. I'm sorry for your loss." I nodded and gave him my phone number. He told me he would call me if he had any leads. I was becoming too familiar with this scene; Jatori, Lex and Lando, and now this. I felt like I was becoming hot, and I needed to cool the fuck off. Bodies were piling up, and I knew eventually the shit would start to look suspicious.

I had to stay until everything cleared. I wanted to play the grieving son role; but in all actuality, I didn't give a fuck. I grabbed all of DJ.'s stuff and left. I passed the blood stain on the carpet and shook my head. I couldn't believe my own father tried to destroy me like that. That shit kinda fucked a nigga up. I called Bella to ask where she was, and she answered quickly.

"Baby, are you ok? Where are you?" Hearing her voice put me at ease.

"I'm leaving the condo; where y'all at?"

"Papa refused to go to the hospital; we're at his house. Peaches is trying to get the bullet out." I could hear Antonio screaming.

"Be there in a minute, aight?"

"Ok, hurry up; love you."

I smiled. "I love you too, Baby."

I drove as fast as I could to get there; my mental was fucked up something serious. I still felt like there was a problem. I couldn't put my finger on it, but something still wasn't right. I made it to Antonio's house and was stuck to Bella the rest of the night. I didn't want to let them out of my sight. Peaches got the bullet out, cleaned the wound with peroxide, and taped a rag over the wound. I was ready to go, so I told Bella to come on.

"I don't want to go back to that place. Let's just got to the beach house." I nodded my head, grabbed DJ.'s car seat, and headed for the door.

"Did you know about what happened to my wife?" Antonio caught me. Bella was staring at me like she was waiting for an answer too.

"He told me when I was young about a woman who was stealing out his stash. He said he chased her off the road, and I put it together when I found out your wife died back then. I didn't know for sure." I twisted the truth a little. I knew it was her, but I didn't want Bella fucked up with me.

"You don't owe me shit, Domo; but you did owe her the truth," he said, nodding his head toward Bella. I saw the tears forming in her eyes, and I knew she was gonna be fucked up with me regardless.

On the drive home, Bella didn't say one word to me. We got to the beach house, and she didn't even wait for me to open the

IN LOVE WITH THE CONNECT 2

door; she got out and grabbed DJ..

"Bella, I didn't want to hurt you again; that's why I didn't want to say anything." I figured I would just say something instead of it being like this.

"Domo, you knew what really happened to my mother this whole time, and you didn't tell me? How do you expect me to trust you if you keep lying to me? You lied about fucking other bitches; you lied about Diamond and the baby. You're just a liar, Domo." That shit cut me deep. I knew then and there that she lost all trust in me.

"So what are you saying?" I asked, starting to feel like I fucked up for good now.

"I don't know; I just think I need some space from you. You knew how my mother's death hurt me, and you couldn't even tell me the truth. I can't trust you anymore." She had tears falling. I went to comfort her and she pushed me away.

"Baby, don't do this shit. Just let me take you in the house and we can talk about this shit."

She shook her head no. "Just leave, Domo. I just need time."

"I want to be here to protect you, even if you don't want me here."

"I can call my father. He's the only man who ever protected me anyway." She must have really wanted me to get mad. I wasn't about to snap on her ass though. I just threw my hands up.

"Aight Bella; if this what you want, fuck it. I'm gone."

I went in the back and grabbed DJ.'s stuff I got from the condo. She walked upstairs to the bedroom, and I thought it was best to just go. She wasn't feeling a nigga right now, and I didn't think I could change her mind. I left out the door feeling like the biggest fool in the world. *I think I just lost my wife.*

Chapter 15

Bella

Six Weeks Later

I was so miserable without Domo. He only came to see DJ., and then he left. I didn't try to talk to him either; I knew he would try and sweet talk me into giving in to him, but not this time. I just felt empty; I was lonely at night, and I wanted him to suffer a little. He didn't even look my way, but I guess I couldn't be too hurt because I'm the one who told him to leave. I don't think I was being irrational just because I wanted honesty from him. He kept lying to me and knew I don't trust him at all. I couldn't let him keep doing this to me. I really did need space and time to think. Look how much he put me through already. I just didn't think I could take any more. I just had to live my life from now on and try to stand on my own two feet. He had a Bentley delivered to the beach house; it held a note on the driver side that said *Happy Birthday*. This must have been one of my gifts. It was gorgeous, and I fell in love with it.

I was going back to the spa next week, and I was so excited. Domo had held up his end of the deal to put the daycare in there. I was happy to take my boo to work with me. I hired six staff members, and it was opening on Monday. I hired a professional service that specialized in setting up schools and child care facilities. I called Domo to thank him, but he didn't answer the phone for me and never called back. As stupid as it sounded, I hoped he wasn't with anybody else. I tried not to think about it, but the more I did the more it drove me crazy. I needed a distraction, and since DJ. was with Domo I called Peaches to hang out.

"Hey, Peaches. What you doing?" I asked, pouring me a glass of wine.

"Nothing, sitting here ready to fuck my little sister up. You know Bizzy got released, right? Tell me why I went to the house to get the rest of my shit because I thought he was still locked up, and I caught them fucking. Can you believe that shit?"

Damn; she was like eighteen or some shit. That nigga was low for that one. It might sound shady, but serves her ass right for doing me like she did.

"What you do, girl?" I said, eager to get all the tea.

"I beat her little ass, and I smashed his ass over the head with one of his high school basketball trophies."

I busted out laughing imagining the scene in my head. "Well, why don't you come over and we can kick it?"

She exhaled deeply. "I'm tired of being in the house. Why we can't go somewhere?"

That made sense; I ain't been out in forever. I went to the closet and looked through some of my latest buys. I had a cute black and yellow halter maxi dress that I was ready to slay in. I had been doing my sit-ups every day, so my stomach was back to being flat as a board.

"Aight. Be here at like ten."

We hung up and I looked at the clock; it was almost nine. I got in the shower and lotioned myself up. I sprayed perfume all over and proceeded to do my hair. I curled it and picked it out with my fingers to give me a full set of spirals. I beat my make up for the gawds and put on my dress. It stopped at my thighs, and I couldn't help but admire myself in the mirror. I looked damn good. I slid into my black stiletto sandals, and I was ready. I looked through my clutches and found a black one with diamonds encrusted around the seam.

I checked my phone for the time, and it was ten thirty. Where the hell was Peaches? I looked out the window, and I saw her walking to the front door with a bottle in her hand. I went to open the door, and I was stunned at how she looked; she was looking like a certified dime piece.

"Damn, Bella; you looking for a new nigga already or something?"

I laughed and let her walk in. "I got some Bacardi. Let's do some shots." I went to the kitchen to get some glasses. She sat the bottle on the island and popped it open. We poured up our shots and took the first one down.

"How you been doing?" she asked, pouring another shot.

"It's hard, but I'm getting through it. I love him so much."

She raised her glass, and we took down the second round. "I know how you feel; y'all gonna work it out."

I shrugged my shoulders. "I don't know, Peaches; I just can't deal with him lying and shit. But you know what? Tonight, we're having fun. I don't want to ruin it." She nodded her head and pulled out a jay.

"You wanna hit this?"

I looked at her like she was crazy. "You know I wanna hit that shit. I been pregnant for eight months." She fired it up. We got right, and were ready to go. We chose to go to Cameo; it was a Saturday night, and we knew it would be jumping.

"I invited my friend to come too; hope that's ok."

I didn't care, as long as she was cool.

"Who is she?" I asked her, pulling up at the light.

"My stylist, remember I told you about her?" I snapped my finger, remembering the conversation we had at the condo.

"Yeah, I remember; I might change it up and get her to do my hair."

"Oh aight. Damn, look at this line," she said, pointing to the club.

"Damn; it must be free or some shit. Let's find somewhere to park."

I found a space seven blocks down. My feet were going to be screaming. We walked down and got cat calls the whole way. Niggas were approaching us left and right. We ignored them all and kept walking. When we got to the door, we decided to cut the line for a hundred dollars. The club was packed when we got inside. We were already lit, so I decided to get a drink later. I just wanted to dance now.

We hit the floor immediately, and we were dancing our asses off. Peaches' phone lit up, so she walked off to answer it. I felt somebody tugging on me, so I turned around and it was this fine ass chocolate dude; he had to be six seven. He was clean cut and had diamonds in his ears.

"Wassup, baby girl," he said, leaning down in my ear. I smiled and couldn't help how sexy this dude was.

"Nothing; just waiting for my friend to come back," I said, trying to get as close to his ear as possible. I slipped and he caught me. His cologne was intoxicating, and I drunk it in.

"Be careful, ma; you almost made a Facebook video. I know people was ready." I laughed, and he flashed his pretty white teeth. "You wanna dance? I'm Jamal, by the way," he said in my ear. I nodded my head yes.

"I'm Bella," I said, trying to scream over the music. It was just dancing; what harm could come of it? We danced for two songs, and we were grinding on each other hard. Peaches came walking back, and she had somebody with her. It was kind of dark, except for the strobe lights and some dim ones. When Peaches walked up and moved aside, I recognized the bitch right away. She knew who I was too, because she was smiling like she won a prize or something.

"Peaches, what the fuck you doing with this bitch? That's Domo's ex. You was setting me up or something?" I pushed Jamal off of me.

"No, I wasn't setting you up. I didn't know what. I met her at the salon, I swear."

"You threatened or something? I mean, obviously your ass got the nigga, so why you mad? Oh, I know why; I heard y'all broke up and you scared I'm gonna pounce on his ass." She started laughing.

"Bitch, please. I could call that nigga right now to eat this pussy and he would come running. You know what? Fuck you; I ain't boutta argue with no looney ass desperate bitch." She stepped forward, and Peaches put her arm in front of her.

"Shay, this my A1, I can't let this shit go down. I'm with her when it comes down to it." Lashay just smiled and pulled out her phone.

"Yeah, let's see how fast he come running," she said, walking away. I went to the bar and got a drink. Peaches walked up behind me.

"You aight, Bella? I swear, I didn't know that was his ex."

I waved my hand. "I know you didn't. Fuck her."

My phone started vibrating. Domo was calling me. I hit the end button. A second later, my phone vibrated. I opened it, and it was a text from him with pictures attached. It was me dancing with the guy. I knew that bitch Lashay did that shit; she was a thirsty ass bitch.

Domo: So that's who you with now? I mean, you said you needed space and you out grinding on some nigga like you ain't still my wife?

This nigga had some nerve.

Me: You didn't care that I was your wife when you were fucking that bitch in France.

Domo: aight Bella; if that's how you want to play it, then that's cool.

I didn't say anything back to that; what the hell did that mean? I called his phone, but it went straight to voicemail. I just continued the rest of my night. I wasn't going to let him stop me from having fun. Me and Peaches turned up the whole night. I went home and crashed as soon as I got in my room. I didn't even get undressed. My ass was lit.

****

The next day, I woke up hung over something serious. My head was pounding and my stomach was hurting. I went to the bathroom and grabbed some Tylenol for my head. I changed into some sweat pants and a t-shirt; I went to the kitchen to see if I had some ginger ale. All I had was orange juice. I drunk some and went back upstairs to lay down; a few minutes later, the door opened and I knew it was Domo; I went downstairs to meet him to get DJ.. He was putting his baby bag down. DJ. was asleep in his car seat.

"Hey," I said, walking into the foyer.

"Wassup," he said, opening the door to leave.

"Domo, wait."

He turned to me with no expression on his face. "Yeah."

"I was just dancing with the guy; I went to—" He stopped me.

"You don't have to explain yourself. You're grown, right? You made it clear you don't want to be with me anymore, so I won't hold you back. I was going to wait, but I decided last night we need a divorce. I can't have my wife out in clubs grinding on niggas and shit. So I will get the papers out to you." He closed the door, and my heart started pounding. I opened it.

"Domo, wait. You want to divorce me? I just told you I needed space," I said on the verge of tears.

"Bella, apparently I can't make you happy; I'm a liar, and I can't protect you. That's what you said to me. That doesn't sound like you're happy, mami." I couldn't stop the tears from falling. He walked up and wiped them from my face.

"Stop it. I'm just trying to do what I think is best for you. I keep breaking your heart, and I see what it's done to you. I love you enough to let you go baby." I couldn't say anything to dispute that.

"I can't believe you gave up on me so fast. I think you're just mad because I was dancing with somebody." The look on his face told me that was the reason.

"You said you don't trust me, baby; how can we be happy if we don't have that? I got what you were saying when you broke up with me. I keep fucking up, and I can't seem to get right." Just then, DJ. started crying.

"Wait, come back inside," I said, running up the steps to get him. I picked him up and when I turned around, Domo was gone. I closed the door and went upstairs. I laid across the bed while DJ. played and squirmed around. Maybe I should just accept it; we were over. I watched my phone all night to see if Domo would call me, and he didn't. I texted Peaches to tell her what happened, and she assured me he was just being a jealous asshole. That gave me no comfort. I watched TV until I fell asleep.

****

It was Monday morning, and after sulking all weekend, I was ready to go back to work. I got DJ. ready, and I was headed out the door. I went to my car and got infuriated. The windows were busted out, and it was keyed up. It was my first day back, and this happens. I couldn't catch a break to save my life. I went in the house to get my keys for my Challenger. I strapped DJ. in and called the insurance company when I got on the road. I knew there was only one ignorant bitch who would do that. I hit Peaches and told her to tell her lil' buddy I was going to stick my whole foot in her ass for fucking up my car. Peaches was pissed off for me and said she was going to call her ass. You don't fuck with nobody shit; she was another one that needed to be taught a lesson. She better hope I didn't come across her, because it was going to go down on sight when I caught her. I pulled up in King of Queen, and grabbed DJ. and his bag. I walked in, and they had balloons and streamers that said *Welcome Back* in bold letters. I looked at the receptionist desk and got sad thinking about Lex. I snapped out of it as everybody was fawning over DJ.. I took him downstairs to the daycare center. There were already children running around playing; I went to the infant room and spoke to all of the employees. It was time to get back into the swing of things.

The day was successful, and I was satisfied with the way things were being run while I was gone. They had been doing great business, and bringing in a lot of money. I decided to keep on my replacement as a secondary. She was amazing; her name was Jackie, and she was a white lady with blond hair. She was beautiful too. I sat in my office and looked around; everything was exactly the same. I heard my ringtone go off, and I grabbed it out of my purse to see if it was Domo; it was my father instead.

"Hola, mi hija."

"Hola Papa. Qué pasa?"

"I see you're speaking more Spanish; you only did that when you're mad about something." I laughed because he was right. When I was angry or sad, I spoke Spanish when I talked to him.

"Ok, is this better?" I said, speaking in English now.

"Whatever you want; anyway, what you doing today? I wanted to come see you guys today." I gathered my purse, put some files in my desk, and cut off the light. One of the daycare workers ran upstairs out of breath.

"What's wrong?" I asked as she tried to catch her breath.

"Some lady came in here and took DJ.." I dropped my phone and ran downstairs, and tore the daycare apart.

"How the fuck could you let somebody take my son!" I screamed at all of them.

"She came in here like she had a child in here. She snatched DJ. from the nursery and ran."

I ran upstairs to get my phone to call Domo. I saw I had a text. It was a picture of DJ. laying on what looked like my comforter from a blocked number. This bitch must be fucking crazy. I dialed Domo, but he didn't answer. I texted him that Lashay took DJ.. I went to look at the security footage while I waited for him to respond. It sure was that bitch. I could see her walk in and talk to the receptionist, then she went downstairs and into the nursery. A minute later, she was running out with DJ., She better not hurt my baby. My phone started ringing, and it was Domo.

"Bella, what the hell Is going on!" he screamed into the phone.

"That bitch ass ex of yours took our son. She grabbed him from the nursery; she sent me a picture of him at the beach house in the bed," I said with tears streaming. I was already in the car doing a hundred to the house.

"I'm on the way there now. I'ma kill that bitch," he said.

"Not before I do."

I hung up and made my way to the house. I went under the flower pot and grabbed the nine we kept under the soil. I opened the door, and I could hear DJ. crying upstairs. I ran up there, and he was laying on the bed screaming his lungs out. I went to get him and he started sucking his fingers. I heard a noise and raised my gun, but it was Domo.

"Where is the bitch?"

I shrugged my shoulders and kissed my baby. "I didn't see her. I just got here." I threw the gun on the bed. He went through the house and she wasn't there. He came back in the room and checked DJ. out.

"Something's always happening; I'm sick of this shit." He took DJ. from me. "I don't want you taking him back there." I couldn't help but agree.

"Do you need security in there or something?" he said, patting DJ.'s back.

"I don't know what to do, Domo. I don't want to let him out of my sight now. Maybe I can keep him in the office with me."

He nodded. "That sounds good, but why don't you just take some more time off?"

"I guess; I don't know, Domo. I just thank God he's ok." I stood next to them and ran my hand over DJ.'s head. Domo looked, and me and our eyes locked. I looked away and went to call ADT. Domo grabbed my arm.

"I was jealous, aight? I'm sorry for threatening to divorce you. That was childish." I gave him a slight grin and went to make my call. They sent people out right away to upgrade the system and install cameras. I changed the code and had a locksmith change the locks. Domo stayed with me the whole time.

"I guess I should be going now." He got up and put DJ. in his crib.

"You wanna spend the night? After today, I really don't want to be alone," I said, hoping he would oblige. He took his shoes off and sat back up on the bed with me. I turned the TV on, and we watched in silence.

"Where's the Bentley?"

I had been so caught up with DJ. being taken that I forgot to tell him about the car.

"Another little gift from your friend. All my windows were busted out, and it was keyed."

He sat up with his eyes squinted. "I paid eight hundred thousand dollars for that fucking car!" I shushed him because he was going to wake the baby up.

"I know, baby; it's in the shop now."

He closed his eyes and tried to calm himself down. "I can buy you another one. I'm sorry she did that shit. She really fucked up in the head."

I nodded in agreement. He moved close to me, and I laid my head on his chest. He kissed the top of my head and wrapped his arms around me. I fell asleep in that position, and shortly after I did I was awakened by my pussy being eaten. I looked down and Domo was between my legs, licking the soul out of me.

"Oh shit; I don't think we should be doing this," I moaned and he squeezed my thighs tighter.

"I do; you still my wife, right?" I grabbed the back of his head and tried not to yank it off his shoulders.

"Oh shit!" I screamed. He put his hand over my mouth.

"Shhhhh. You're gonna wake DJ. up."

He went back to making circles on my clit. I gripped the bed sheets and enjoyed the backflips his tongue was making my clit do. I couldn't hold it anymore, and I came so hard my toes were cracking. He got up and started kissing my neck. He lifted my shirt over my head, removing it. He stuck his tongue in my mouth, and I could taste myself on his face and lips. He made his way to my nipples and flicked his tongue as he sucked each one; I was more than ready for that dick.

"You want this.?" he said, getting up, pulling his pants down, and stroking his pole. My mouth was watering as I nodded yes. He took his jeans completely off and got between my legs. They were shaking with anticipation.

"Tell me, baby," he said, kissing on my chest and running his fingers through my hair.

"I want it, daddy."

He put the head in and stopped. "How much? Tell me how much you want me to in this pussy," he said, poking the head in and out, driving my ass crazy.

"I want you to have this pussy, Domo; put it in, baby."

He pushed it all in, and my mouth was in an 'o' shape be- cause I was so tight from not having sex; I felt like he busted me open. He was digging for gold in me; it felt so good that I wanted to cry.

"Oh my God, baby!" I said screamed, scratching his back up.

"Fuck; I missed your ass, girl," he said, biting his bottom lip and looking down at me.

"I missed you too, baby," I said, enjoying this good eggplant he was giving me. When he got back up, I screamed and began punching him in the face. It was Domo's father on top of me. I kicked and fought.

"Baby, wake up!"

I looked around, and it was morning. Domo had on a t-shirt and boxers, and I still had all my clothes on. It must have been a dream.

"I'm sorry; I was having a nightmare."

He kissed my forehead. "It must have been a good one. You was whooping my ass just now." He laughed and smiled.

"Yeah; we were having sex."

He raised his eyebrows. "That was a nightmare to you?"

I shook my head no. "You turned into a monster," I said, leaving out the fact his father was the monster.

"Well, did I hit it right?"

I pushed his shoulder and stood up. "Thank you for staying with us last night," I said, looking into DJ.'s crib.

"You don't have to thank me; I love y'all." I turned to him.

"We love you too, Domo," I said, really wanting to say *I love you and come get this pussy, daddy.*

"I know you do. I gotta go; do you need anything before I

leave?" I shook my head no and sat back down.

"Where you staying?" I asked him; he never told me where he went the night he left.

"At the condo; had to get the carpet cleaned," he said, pulling off his shirt. Damn, he had a body like a Greek God. His six-pack was tight, and his arms were muscled up. I looked back up to him, and he was staring at me smiling.

"Don't act like you ain't seen it before."

I blushed and went into the bathroom. I didn't have to do shit; I just wanted to be away from him before I fucked his brains out. I didn't want to send him mixed signals, so I thought it was best we didn't have sex at all. He tapped on the door and I went to open it.

"I'm leaving; we don't have to not talk. You can call me, Bella." I felt the tears welling up. I hated that I was such a damn crybaby. Of course, like his sweet self always did, he wiped them before they could fall down my face.

"I will."

He gripped my chin and pulled me to his face, and I let him kiss me. I never knew how much I missed that until just now. He left and I sat in my room alone again. I went looking through my pictures in my phone, and looked at us smiling and happy. I wanted love, but I didn't want to be stupid for it. I put up with so much from him already, and I kept thinking it would only get worse the longer I stayed. I wanted Domo to realize what he had so we didn't have to keep going through this same shit over and over again. I just wanted to be happy and in love. Was that too much to ask? I didn't think so.

****

After being holed up in the house for three days, I was running out of food. I needed to get milk for DJ. too. I grabbed my purse and headed out the door, and strapped DJ. into his car seat. I started driving to the super Walmart. They had a full grocery section, and they weren't overpriced like most places. I walked up and down the freezer aisle picking up nothing but junk. I loved ice cream, so I stood there forever trying to make a choice. I finally picked up the Ben and Jerry's strawberry cheesecake one.

"That's my favorite one."

I jumped because the voice scared me; it was so deep. I turned to see the guy from the club the other night. Jamal.

"Oh hi; how you doing?"

He gave me a big Coca-Cola smile. "Better now that I ran into you. You ain't boutta be fighting nobody up in here, are you?"

I laughed and closed the freezer door. "Nah; I put my gloves up for the day."

"Is this your little man?"

I nodded my head yes, smiling with pride at my baby. "Yes; his name's DJ.."

He leaned into the cart. "Hey DJ.; you hanging with mommy today?" He stood back up. "So since you ran off on me at the club, I didn't get a chance to ask you if you had a man?" I knew it was coming.

"I'm married. My husband and I are kind of separated right now," I told him; it stung to even say that.

"Well, that means I can take you out, right?" I shook my head no.

"I'm not looking for anything right now. We're going to work it out." He looked disappointed. I could tell that wasn't what he wanted to hear.

"You know you just hurt my feelings, right?" He started pouting and poking his lip out. "Do this then. Take my number and I'ma call you, aight? Ain't no harm in talking." I felt like this was a bad idea.

"I will call you," I said, pulling out my phone. He punched his number in, and I saved it with no name.

"Why don't you text me and I can save yours." I put my phone in my back pocket.

"Nope." I walked off.

"You gonna do me like that, baby?"

I kept walking and smiled all the way around the corner. He so sexy, but I didn't want to get myself in any shit that I couldn't get out of. When I got home, I couldn't stop thinking about Jamal.

His smile was forever plastered in my head. Later that night, I kept going over it in my mind. I didn't have to go out with him; I could just use him for conversation. I went to my contacts and clicked the number.

"I knew you would call me, beautiful."

Peaches

"Oh shit, Papi!"

Antonio was tearing this pussy up. I had my legs up behind my head, and he was taking full advantage of the position. He was finally healed up from that gunshot wound, and he was trying to rip my ass apart now that he could stroke without pain. He flipped me over and went into me from the back. He grabbed my hair and I popped his hand. I didn't play with that shit. He knew that. He started fucking me harder, I guess to punish me. I threw that ass back at him to show him Peaches could take the dick. He smacked my ass hard several times, and he pulled out and nutted on my ass.

"Damn; you got my legs trembling, girl," he said, walking to the bathroom and coming back with a rag to wipe me off.

"You know how this pussy works, Papi," I said, standing up and kissing him on the lips.

"What you got planned for today?" he asked, pulling his underwear up.

"Nothing. Still trying to get in contact with my mother." I hadn't spoken to my mom since she left. She wouldn't return any of my phone calls or text. I didn't know what she was thinking not letting me check on my kids.

"Do you want me to look for her? You know I got connections everywhere."

"You know what? Yeah. That's a good idea. I'm sure she's at

IN LOVE WITH THE CONNECT 2

her sister's house, but I don't have the number."

"Ok, I got you," he said, kissing my cheek. I was ecstatic to be back with Antonio; A few days after I checked into that hotel, he called to check on me. He said he broke things off with his girl, or should I say *woman friend*, and he wanted to come chill with me. I didn't see what he saw in her anyway, and I probably never would.

"Aight, I'll see you later," he said, walking out the door.

"Ok." He winked at me and left.

I needed to get in the shower and get this fuck sweat off me. I put on Pandora, then sat in the tub and soaked. I started thinking about how I wanted to call my sister to see if she was ok; I may have beat her ass, but I still wanted to make sure Bizzy ain't fuck her up.

"What you want?" she said, answering the phone with an attitude.

"Don't get fucked up, Anna. I was calling to see if your trifling ass was ok."

She smacked her lips. "Don't worry about me, my man got this. You just mad that the best bitch won."

She sounded so dumb. "What did you win? A free ass whooping and some mediocre dick? You know what? You ain't even worth the trouble. Don't call me when he beating your ass." I just lied my ass off, and I'm sure she knew it' Bizzy had that strong long.

"Don't worry, I ain't a weak bitch like you and your dumb ass friends. I know what it takes to please a nigga so he won't want to hit me when I'm done."

I laughed her ass out. "Bitch bye."

I hung up on her simple ass; she had no idea what she was getting herself into with this nigga. If she wanted to be dumb and not take heed, then that was on her ass. I finished my bath and got dressed for the day. I chose a pair of high-waisted jean shorts and a pink bustier. I looking bomb, and I threw on a pair of pink and white Jordans to match. I was going to make a quick stop by Bella's house before I went and got this tree from Lova. I went to her contact and hit call.

"Hey Peaches, wassup."

"I'm good; I was boutta stop through there and chill for a minute." I heard a man's voice in the background. I couldn't tell if it was Domo or not.

"I'm out right now. I'll call you when I get home so we can chill." She didn't even wait for me to say anything; she just hung up.

I said fuck it and just went to meet up with Lova. She told me to meet her at her grandmother's house because she hurt her ankle. When I got to the door, I knocked and I could hear somebody slowly walking to the door. It slowly opened, and Lova had a cast on her ankle, and she had one crutch.

"Aaaaaw poor baby," I said, teasing her as she hopped to the back of the house; I knew this was her room. It looked like what a nigga's room was supposed to look like; she had posters of basketball, rappers, and some more shit everywhere.

"Go in that shoe box on the top right, and grab what you need," she said, sitting down on the bed.

"How you do that?" I said, pointing at her cast.

"I was trying to talk to this lil' shawty and twisted it stepping off the curb."

"You always chasing pussy; finally caught up to you, huh?"

She grinned and watched me open the bag to smell the weed. "You know I never got over your ass, right? I don't know why you act like we wasn't poppin'." This is why I always kept it short with her. She always brought up our old thing.

"I'm not gay, Lova; I was horny, and you ate pussy better than my nigga. You act like we were dating and shit."

She lit up a blunt and gave it to me. "I wasn't saying all that, but you know you used to be pressed to come get licked out."

I passed the blunt back to her, exhaling my smoke. "Whatever you say. I gotta roll though."

She sat up and pulled me back down. "How 'bout one for old time's sake?"

I smirked at her and pushed her away. "No, because you're

never gonna leave me alone if I let you."

She got up and rubbed my ass, and it was making me feel some type of way.

"Just one more taste; it ain't gon' hurt you to cum."

I thought about it, and since Antonio said he wasn't ready to jump back in all the way, I was single and able to do what I pleased.

"Your ankle all fucked up and you worried about eating me out."

She laid down and scooted to the middle of the bed. "Ride my face; I wanna catch all that sweet cream."

I pulled my shorts down and climbed on the bed over top of her. She stopped me to unstrap my bustier so she could see my titties. she squeezed and put sloppy kisses all over them and started to suck on my nipples, and I started creaming right away. I stopped her and proceeded to sit on her face. Her thick tongue was stiff as I bounced on it, and the shit was making my muscles tighten. She spread my ass cheeks so she could go deeper, and I leaned forward and gripped the bed.

"Yeees Lova. Eat this pussy."

I started grinding her face harder until my cum ran down, glazing her face like a donut. My legs were shaking and I was stuck in that same position for a minute.

"I see you been eating those piiiiineapples," she said, laughing as she still lay under me imitating Usher.

"You know I like to keep it tasting sweet." I got up and it was sticky between my legs.

"I need to wash up."

She nodded her head to the door. "The bathroom's down the hall; you can get a rag and towel out the closet."

I went and took a whole shower; I couldn't put the same underwear on so I went without them. I knew it was rude, but I walked straight out the door so not even saying bye to Lova. She would only try to press me out to lick it again.

I sped off and headed back home so I could chill until Bella called to get together. I heard my text tone go off, so I unlocked my phone and saw it was from Lova. She said it was fucked up that I came in her mouth and left. I laughed and didn't even respond. I made my way back home and texted Antonio to tell him I was back. He lived about ten minutes away from me. I never let go of the house I moved into when I left Bizzy, so I just moved right back in. He came over a lot, but he didn't want to make us official again just yet. I didn't fight him on it either; I just accepted it. I was happy to even have a piece of him.

I called my mom's phone again, and it was still going to voicemail. I guess I just had to wait to see if Antonio could find her. I missed my babies so much; I just wanted to talk to them and hear their voices. I sat back on the couch and let my mind wander.

****

A few hours later I was smoking and watching Martin; basically chilling my ass off. My phone started ringing, and I was irritated when I saw Bizzy's name.

"What Bizzy!" I yelled into the phone.

"Open the door, I wanna talk to you." My heart started beating so fast. I ran to the room and grabbed the gun I kept on the top shelf.

"Bizzy, I'm warning your ass to get the hell outta here." I looked through the peephole and saw him with his phone in his hand.

"Peaches, I'm not going to hurt you; just let me talk to you for a minute. I promise, I won't bother you again after today if you don't want me to."

I didn't know why, but I felt like he was being sincere. I wasn't a fool though, so I still didn't open the door.

"You can say whatever you have to say. I'm right here." I watched him make a frustrated face through the peephole.

"Aight, look; I know what you did Peaches, and I know it sounds dumb as shit for a nigga to say, but I'm glad you did it."

I knew he was talking about the call I made to the police about the weight he had in his car. I had to do something to get him to leave me alone. They didn't hold him because he must have already taken the shit out before they got to him. He only got caught with two vials of dope and a few ecstasy pills.

"Why are you doing this, Bizzy? You think I'm stupid? The moment I open the door, you're going to fuck me up and you know it."

"Peaches, when I got arrested, they had to take me to the infirmary because I was throwing up blood. They said it may have been the liquor, but they were checking me for internal bleeding. Few days later, they found out I had stomach cancer and I only have a year to live. So I was just saying thank you for the good shit you gave me in my life. Even though Marcus was Drew's, I raised him like my own. Yeah, it was fucked up how you did me, but I still wanted to be with your ass. Regardless of what you think, I did love you and still do; I just had a fucked up way of showing it. Tell the kids I love them too," he said, starting to walk away.

I honestly didn't know how to feel. I thought about all the shit we went through, and it made it hard to be emotional about this. He just called a few weeks ago threatening me and my family. He beat my ass day in and day out, and he wanted me to feel sorry for him? He was fucking my little sister, and I was supposed to shed a fucking tear? I still had a certain amount of love for him, but I couldn't let him suck me back in because he was sick. I would have to be an idiot. I was an idiot; I was a stupid bitch to be exact because I unlocked the door and tucked the gun in the back of my shorts.

"Bizzy," I called to him. He turned around with a smile on his face. He looked at me like he used to do when he saw me; like was the only person on the earth. He had tears in his eyes.

"I'm scared, Peaches," he said. I walked to him, and he put his arms out for a hug. I went to embrace him, and he squeezed me tightly. He started crying, and I embraced him and let him cry on my shoulder.

"I swear, I'm sorry for everything, baby. I love you, girl."

I stayed in his embrace, but I didn't say it back. "What are you going to do? I mean, do you have a doctor or something? I can go with you if you need somebody," I said, finally letting go of the hug.

"Yeah, I'm supposed to be going to chemo; not that they said it would help." He didn't treat me the best all the time, but he was still the father of my children.

"Aight, well call me if you need anything," I said, backing away from him.

"Can I come in for a minute?" I was hesitant, but I had my gun just in case he started some shit.

"Why? I still don't trust your ass, Bizzy."

He put his hand on his chest. "After eight years, you can't tell when I'm being genuine?"

I squinted my eyes and pursed my lips. "Come on." I walked in, and he came in behind me. As soon as he closed the door, he grabbed me by my hair, but not in a rough way. He pulled my face to his and started kissing me. I pushed him off.

"Bizzy, I just caught you fucking my sister. I can't fuck with you like that no more." He wasn't hearing me, and he tried to kiss me again. I slapped him, and he didn't even get mad.

"You want it rough, huh?"

He was still fine as hell; he was light brown with a nice build. He had a perfect smile, and one dimple on the left cheek. When he said that, I got turned on remembering how we used to fuck like animals. I couldn't. I opened the door.

"Leave, Bizzy."

He slammed it and cupped my face, and kissed me harder. I was fighting him, but he pressed his full weight on me, and I was pinned between him and the wall. He started kissing my neck and I stopped fighting. Call me what you want, but I was getting the dick and he could go. I felt a little like a hoe because I fucked Antonio earlier, got head from Lova, and now I was about to fuck Bizzy.

"I missed you, Peaches; even when I wanted to kill you, I still wanted you," he said, pulling my shorts down. The gun hit the floor hard, and he looked down at it. "You always been my gangsta bitch."

He lifted me up, and my legs wrapped around him. He held

me with one hand while he unbuckled his belt and pulled his dick out. He slid it into me, and I slid down that shit; my legs started shaking immediately. He had me against the wall with my legs wide open and pussy dripping wet. You could hear the gushing sounds while he was hitting my spot.

"Damn, Bizzy; make me cum, baby."

He started pounding harder, and I pulled my legs back and came all on his dick. He wasn't done yet. He carried me across the living room with his dick still inside me.

"Ride this dick for me, baby."

He turned and sat on the couch, and he started moving me up and down. I pushed his hands behind his head and started bouncing my ass on him until I came a second time. He was stroking me for dear life. My eyes were tightly closed, enjoying the pain and pleasure he was giving me. When I opened them, my heart almost flew out of my chest. Antonio was standing there with one of his boys.

"Stop Bizzy."

"Nah ma, this pussy too good right now," he said. I wanted to bust his ass in the head with the lamp.

"Antonio—" Bizzy stopped and turned around. He smiled at Antonio, and he started stroking me again. I jumped off him.

"Antonio, I'm sorry—"

"You sure are; let's get out this trick's spot, man." I grabbed my clothes and started putting them on to catch Antonio before he left.

"Antonio, wait!" I screamed, running to the car. He looked at me as he bolted off down the street. I fucked up again. I had to be the dumbest bitch in the world. I walked back in the house feeling like a complete idiot. Bizzy had his pants back on, and he was sitting on the couch watching TV.

"I guess we got you in trouble, huh?" he said, looking at me with a satisfied expression.

"Bye Bizzy, just leave. You caused enough trouble."

He stood up and grabbed me by the waist. "Can you come back home? I want you and the kids to come back." I started getting angry, because this nigga was the reason they weren't here. I was sitting here fucking him and shit, and my kids are gone and I couldn't even talk to them. Damn, I felt like a stupid ass hoe.

"No, Bizzy. We ain't no good together. Did you forget you threatened me? What if you start doing that drinking and shit and beat me to death? I can't." He nodded his head ok.

"Aight then." He walked past me, and my phone started ringing. I looked and saw it was Anna. Fine time to call now. I heard the door close, so I knew Bizzy had left.

"Yeah Anna," I said, sitting on the couch.

"Peaches, you need to get the fuck out of Miami. I just got loose from the basement; Bizzy tied me up and locked me down there." My chest started pounding.

"What the fuck are you talking about? Bizzy just left here saying he was sick, and the doctor told him he had cancer. He said he wanted to make shit right because he didn't have long." *What the fuck have I done?*

"I been down here for three hours. He sick? Yeah, he sick in his fucking head. He lied to you, Peaches. He's crazy; you need to get the hell out of there." I jumped up and went to the foyer to grab my gun. It was gone.

"Looking for this?" I turned to see Bizzy with the gun pointed to my head.

"I fucking hate you! Why—"

I was cut off by the first bullet tearing through my leg." I dropped the phone and fell down. I could hear Anna calling my name through it. Bizzy came and stood over top of me.

"I wasn't lying, Peaches; I do love you. I just can't let you live without me."

He let off two more shots into my stomach.

"I hate you," I was able to get out before I stopped breathing.

Chapter 16

Domo

I got a frantic call from Bella a few days ago about Peaches; she was rushed to the hospital after being shot four times. She still hadn't woken up from the coma that she had been in for two weeks already. I planned on being by Bella the whole way but she had been acting even more distant lately, and I was starting to feel like she really didn't want to get back together at all. When I saw the picture of dude grinding on her, I got infuriated and almost broke my phone. I looked at the picture again that night and noticed how familiar the guy looked. I couldn't put my finger on it, but I felt like I knew him from somewhere. That bitch Lashay sent me the picture; I went back to that salon I saw her about to go in, but they said she was no longer working there. She put her hands on my son, and for that shit she was going to fall. I tried to be nice to her, but she didn't want that. She wanted the savage to come out, and she got her wish. I was burying her ass as soon as I could.

I went to the hospice I put my mother so I could check on her. She was doing bad, and they didn't think she had much longer to live. My sister had been there for her every day, and I came a few days out the week. When I got up to the room, she was sitting on the bed reading a bible.

"Hey, Dominic. Did you hear the good news?"

I shook my head no. "What is it?" I asked, sitting in the chair next to her.

"Your sister finally got rid of that fool. She got him locked up after he tried to hit her again. She said this time, is was over." She smiled, and most of her teeth were missing.

"That good, Ma," I said, sitting back.

"You ok, boy?"

"Nah, Ma. I fucked up with Bella; She ain't trying to take a nigga back. I don't know what to do." I felt lost without her.

"Well, you put yourself in this situation, I'm sure. You gotta love a woman the way she loves you. Your father fucked your mind up, and now you don't know how to be a good man. You gotta give her time; I know she loves you. She came and shot my ass to protect your little sister."

I laughed trying to picture her doing that shit. "You right. I was a fucked up nigga, and I deserve what's happening right now. I love her to death."

She waved her hand for me to come to her. "God will bring her back to you if he wants y'all to be together. You can't be like your father no more; be like Dominic," she said, rubbing her hand down the back of my head. I decided to just go tell her how I felt, and that I wanted to get back together. I couldn't take not being with her anymore. I sat there a few more minutes with Ma, then I rolled out.

I called Bella's phone, but she didn't answer. I felt my phone vibrate, and it was text from Bella saying she would call me back. I thought that was odd, but whatever. I was hungry as hell, and I needed to eat. I made the twenty-minute drive to Hot Off The Grill; that was me and Bella's favorite place to go. I was going to get some to-go shit because I didn't want to eat alone. I walked to the receptionist and was about to tell her I wanted to get some food to-go when I looked to the right, and knew I was going to jail. Bella was with the nigga who was in the club picture. I walked over, probably looking like a bull that was about to charge. I looked to see if DJ. was over there and he wasn't. She saw me and stood up, backing away from the table. I picked up a glass from off a random table and smashed that nigga over the head with it.

"Domo, what the hell are you doing?" Bella screamed.

"Where the fuck is DJ. while you out here on dates and shit? You asked me not to divorce you just so you can still be fucking with other niggas?" The punk motherfucker was on the floor rolling around. I gave him a swift kick to the stomach.

"Domo, please stop. We're just friends." That made me even madder. I pulled out my gun, and people started running out.

"Don't kill me, man. It wasn't my idea." I squinted my eyes; what wasn't his idea?

"You fucking my wife, nigga?" I asked with the gun to his head. He was shaking. "Don't be scared. She fine as a muthafucka, ain't she? Ain't she!" I screamed. He didn't say shit. "You saying my wife ain't bad, nigga?"

"No—she fine, ok? Yeah, she fine." I smacked him in the head with the gun.

"Bella, this you now? This why you been acting so cold to me, huh?"

"Domo, just leave him alone."

I heard police sirens, so I put my gun up. I couldn't believe she was defending another nigga in my face. Fuck this shit.

"You know what? You right, Bella. She all yours, nigga." I turned to walk away, not even bothering to look back. I was met with police and guns drawn.

"Get down now!" I put my hands up and dropped to the ground on my knees.

"Domo!" Bella screamed.

"Stay right there, ma'am," one of the officers told her.

"That's my husband."

I gritted on her when she said that. "Ex-husband. Her new nigga in there laid out on the floor like a bitch!" I yelled out. They came and cuffed me, and took my gun. As they drove me away, I saw Bella outside the restaurant crying, and I watched her until she disappeared out of sight. I couldn't even think straight, and gave no fucks about being locked up. It was a good thing they got me before I could do any more stupid shit. I knew I fucked up when I thought about the effect this would have on my business. I had clients who are millionaires, and it's one thing for them to not know about my drug business, but for me to get locked up on a gun charge? I just hoped they didn't find out.

I got processed, and they charged me with disturbing the peace and assault. I called my lawyer as soon as I got a call. He told me Bella already called him and told him what happened. I wouldn't be able to see a judge for at least four days. It was Friday, and Memorial day was Monday. I was about to be sitting in this motherfucka. I knew my lawyer was a beast, and I wouldn't get nothing but a slap on the wrist for this shit. He would come up with some way of making this shit go away. The first few hours, I tortured myself with thoughts of Bella fucking that fluke ass nigga. I still couldn't pinpoint who this nigga was but even at the restaurant, I couldn't shake the familiar vibe I had. I would figure the shit out eventually.

****

Four days seem like four months in this bitch. I was hungry as shit, and the scraps they were giving me wasn't shit. I was granted a bond, and I called Lando to get him to come post it. I hadn't talked to him since that day I went to see him. He was ready to come back to work, and he told me he was sorry for what his father did. It wasn't his fault, so he didn't have shit to be sorry about. Lando must have come through with the cash, because I was walking out the door right now. I saw him leaning on his car when I got out front.

"What's up, my nigga!" he yelled, smiling as I walked down the steps. I dapped him up.

"A nigga ready to eat, cuz."

He stood up and looked behind me. "Handle your business, nigga. I'ma be in the whip." I turned around, and Bella was there with DJ..

"What you doing here? Shouldn't you be nursing that nigga?"

She rolled her eyes. "Nothing happened with me and him. We're just friends, Domo." I wasn't trying to hear that shit. That nigga wanted more than friendship.

"Ok, well what's up. I'm boutta head home, man. I been locked up for four days and I wanna get my shit together."

"So we're just not going to talk about it at all?"

I shook my head no and shrugged my shoulders. "Ain't nothing to talk about. You made your choice the other night. I was calling you that night to come talk, and you told me you was busy; then I see you smiling all in ole boy face. How you think that make me look out here, Bella?"

"How you think you made me look, Domo? Oh, you get a pass and shit though, huh?"

I wasn't trying to make excuses for myself, but I'd been keeping myself good for her.

"You right; I fucked up, but I was being faithful after the last time. I ain't so much as look at another bitch."

I saw my lawyer coming down the steps, so I waved him over. "Hey, Mr. Birkdale. I'm confident I can make this go away. No cameras and nobody's talking. The only thing is the gun."

I waved him off. "We don't have to send it; give them to her now."

He pulled the divorce papers I had him draw up while I was locked up. She took the paper and scanned them.

"Domo, we don't have to do this." She looked like she was about to break down.

"You want to see other people, and I don't want to stop you from living your life. Sign them and send them to him. I already signed."

She flipped the pages and found the signatures. I kissed DJ. and got in the car. I didn't want to leave her there like that, but it was best for her. My mother said that if God wanted us together, then he would bring her back. He didn't though; he sent her to another nigga, and if that's what she wanted then I wouldn't stand in her way.

"You good, my nigga?" Lando asked, turning onto the freeway.

"Yeah, I'ma be good. She talking to some other nigga and

shit," I said, in my feelings.

"Damn; we gotta go get this nigga or something?"

I shook my head no. "Nah, fuck that nigga. I know this nigga from somewhere, bruh. I can't think of where though," I said, still trying to figure the shit out.

"What the nigga look like?" I pulled out my phone and went to the text message. I turned the phone to him, and he squinted his eyes and raised his eyebrows.

"Nigga, that's Lil' mal." I was looking at him as if to say, *ok from where*? "Jamal, nigga; remember that nigga Tayvon? The one who was smashing Lashay's cousin. That's his lil' brother."

I snapped my fingers. "Oh yeah, nigga just a little older now. Speaking of Lashay, you heard from that bitch?"

"Nah, I ain't heard from her. I can't believe that bitch kidnapped your son though. I ain't know she was off like that."

I shook my head. "I can't wait to put my hands on her dope head ass. You think that shit with Bella and ole boy is too much of a coincidence?"

He shrugged his shoulders. "I don't know, nigga; won't you go find the nigga." I sat back and thought about it. Nah; it probably wasn't shit but a *by chance* thing.

"Let's go get a nigga some food, bruh; a nigga losing weight already." I tried to act like I was good, but I couldn't get this shit out my mind. Something wasn't right.

Bella

I sat on the bed staring at the divorce papers Domo gave me a few weeks ago. He sent his sister to get DJ. now, and I thought he was being a little over dramatic. I refused to sign the papers, and I even sent them back to the lawyer's office unsigned, but he just sent them again. He couldn't make me sign them, so I would just keep them until he talked to me. I was still talking to Jamal, and he was really a good guy. He said it wasn't my fault that my ex was crazy. I only went out with him two times, but we talked on the phone a lot. I was feeling guilty, but I didn't see anything wrong with having a friend. Domo was apparently done anyway, so what was I supposed to do—roll over and die?

I was up at the hospital to see Peaches. Her condition hadn't changed since she had been brought in. The police were now looking for Bizzy. Anna told them that she heard him right before he shot her. I hoped they caught that bastard.

I walked in, and it always made feel down when I saw all the tubes everywhere. I put the vase of flowers that I just brought for her down on the table. DJ. was sleeping peacefully, so I was able to sit and talk to her like I did every time I came. I didn't know if she could hear me or not, but I did it anyway.

"Hey, Peaches. Girl, I gotta tell you what happened with me and Domo. I was out with the guy we met at the club. Yeah, I know you mad I didn't tell you. Anyway, Domo came in and fucked him up, and now he wants a divorce. I wish you could respond to me. I need to know if I should just let him go. I don't want to." I laid my head on the bed rail.

I was sitting there for almost an hour talking when Peaches' mother came in with the kids.

"Hi Aunt Bella," Marcus said, running over to me.

"Hey, my little cuties." Peaches' mother walked over and looked at her, shaking her head.

"I told this fool to leave that man alone a long time ago." I didn't even respond. Her daughter was laid up in the bed on life support, and she was calling her a fool.

"I have to go, can y'all let me know if anything happens?" She nodded.

I didn't want to be in there with her; she always had a nasty disposition since the first time I met her. I left the hospital and realized I had nothing to do. I decided it was always nice to go shopping. I drove to Dolphin mall. I pulled out the stroller from the trunk and put DJ. in it. I grabbed his bag and tucked it under the stroller. I went into a few stores, but I didn't see anything that caught my eye. I loved shoes, so I went to see if I could get some more sandals. When I walked in Steve Madden, I knew I was about to drop some dough. I started trying on every shoe I thought was cute.

After I was done in there, I had four bags and no way of carrying them out. One of the guys offered to take them to the car for me. I told him that when I came back, he could do it. I didn't want to have to walk all the way back and forth. I went to Calvin Klein next, and while I was looking at some shirts, I saw Domo standing at the jewelry stand. I went to go surprise him when this bitch walked up and put her hand on his back. I was right behind him, and he didn't even know it. She turned and looked at me and I tried to walk away before Domo noticed, but I ran into a rack in the store and made too much noise. He turned around and walked up, trying to help me get the stuff up.

"Hey, Bella; look at my little man," he said, picking DJ. up. The girl he was with walked over to us.

"Hi, I'm Carmen," she said, sizing me up. She ain't have shit on me.

"Bella." I went to grab DJ. back, and Domo turned from me.

"Damn, I can't hold him?" I looked at him, and then the broad, and just walked to some shirts like I was looking for something. I saw him walking up out the corner of my eye.

"Here you go," he said, passing DJ. back to me.

"That's your girl, huh? I see you move just as fast as me, apparently."

He rolled his eyes into the air. "Whatever. You the only one that get to move on?" I swallowed hard when he said that.

"So that's you moving on?"

He nodded his head yeah. "I gotta go; I'm sending Charlene to get him this weekend," he said, backing away. He went and put his hand on the girl's back, and they walked out and kept looking at the jewelry. She picked up a tennis bracelet and tried it on. She jumped up and down when Domo pulled money out, and when I saw her kiss him, I had the urge to slap her ass. *You know what? Fuck this.* I walked up to him.

"I'm sending those papers back today; this time, they will be signed." I took off my ring that I was still wearing and threw it at him. "Go to hell, Domo."

I walked away, leaving the cashier behind me with my bags. I went down the escalator and saw Domo bend down and pick up my ring. He watched me go all the way down. When I got into the car, I was hitting the steering wheel. *You know what? Cool.* Since DJ. was going to be gone, I was going out with Jamal.

I drove home in complete silence. I didn't even turn the radio on; I was alone with my thoughts, and I didn't have a clue what the hell happened to my life. I called my father to talk, but he didn't answer the phone. I didn't know what was wrong with him lately; he hadn't really been around. He told me he just needed to fall back; he hadn't even been up to the hospital to see Peaches. I had a text message, so I opened my phone when I parked at home and it was from Jamal.

Jamal: I miss you pretty, lady; call me.

I clicked his contact. "Hey Jamal," I said, sort of happy to hear from him.

"Nothing, what you up to?"

"On the way home. I went to the mall and bought some shoes," I said, getting out the car.

"You stay shopping. Can I come over tonight?"

He knew he didn't come over my house. I may not have been with Domo, but I wouldn't disrespect his house by fucking another nigga in it. I grabbed DJ. and left all the shoes in the trunk.

"You know that's a dead issue. We can go out this weekend," I said, opening the front door and walking in, happy to sit DJ.'s heavy tail down.

"Ok, that's cool; where you wanna go?" he asked, sounding disappointed.

"I don't know, surprise me," I giggled into the phone.

"Ok, I like that. I hope I can surprise you in other ways too."

I didn't want anything sexual, and I knew that's what he was getting at.

"You better lotion up," I said laughing.

"Damn, that's cold. I'ma call you later, aight?" he said, sounding like he was rushing me off the phone now.

"Ok, that's cool."

After we hung up, I went and got the divorce papers. I read them over, and he was giving me over ten million dollars, and a monthly child support payment of fifty thousand dollars. It also said he purchased a residence for us, and we could move in when the divorce was final. I put my hand on my forehead and just did it. I signed the papers and put them back in the envelope. I sat it on the table so I could take it to the mailbox when I went back outside. I guessed this was it.

****

Friday had come, and I was excited for my date with Jamal. I was waiting for Charlene to come pick DJ. up, and she was running late. I called her phone, and she answered on the first ring.

"I know; I'm coming, Bella," she said without me even having to ask.

"Ok, I was just wondering." I hung up, and a few minutes later she was at the door.

"Hey Bella," she said walking in.

"Wassup. How's everything?" I asked, strapping DJ. into his car seat.

"Everything's ok, just chilling. I started working at Domo's building now. I do custodial though; he didn't think I was professional enough." I hated to hear his name because it hurt.

"Oh ok."

She picked up on my facial expression. "You know he only messing with that girl just because he lonely. I think he still loves you, Bella."

I rolled my eyes. "Well, he has a funny way of showing. it Those are the divorce papers he wants me to hurriedly get back to his lawyer," I said, pointing to the envelope that I still hadn't sent off.

"He is just feeling some type of way about that dude." I didn't care what is was anymore; he had a girl now apparently, so I wasn't about to chase his ass.

"Yeah I guess; well I'm boutta head out soon; be careful driving with my baby," I said, holding the door open.

"He does still love you, Bella; I know him."

"Bye, Charlene," I said, closing the door.

Why the hell did she have to bring him up? I went upstairs to get ready for my date. I didn't know where we were going, but I knew I could wear a dress because Miami was always hot as hell anyway. I put on a short-jumper and a pair of my new shoes. I accessorized and did my makeup. I was ready. I took a few pictures for Facebook and posted a bunch of different positions. I got instant likes, including Domo. I locked my phone back and rolled a jay to get loose. I smoked until my eyes were chinky. Jamal wanted me to meet him on Ocean Drive. He said to just stand by the Versace mansion. I left the house on foot because I didn't live far from there.

When I walked up, I saw him already waiting for me. He looked so good; *damn*.

"Girl, you know you wrong for wearing that. You got a nigga drooling over here."

I smiled and went up to hug him. "How are you?"

He was still holding me tight. "I'm better now. Let's go." He grabbed my hand and pulled me to his side.

"So, you must have figured a place out," I said, walking close to him.

"Yeah; it's a little juvenile, but I think we can have some fun."

We walked down the street until we stopped at Wet Willies. I loved this place, and I was ready to get nice and drunk.

"Can we get two supermen's?" he asked the bartender.

"How you know that's what I wanted?" I said, smiling at him.

"I don't know; I just thought you might like it." I did love them.

When we got our drinks, we sat at the table and talked for a little bit about everything. I genuinely enjoyed his company, and he seemed to be enjoying mine.

"Where do you work?" I realized we never really talked about what he did for a living.

"I do a little of this and a little of that. I dabble in a lot of stuff." That was vague.

"Ugh, ok; that's not really telling me anything."

He finished his drink and went to order two more. He seemed like he was being secretive or something. I was scrolling through my phone until he walked back up.

"Let's take some pictures," I said, turning my camera on.

"Nah; I don't really like pictures, ma." I shrugged my shoulder and took a selfie, then uploaded it. He was watching me the whole time.

"I can't believe he let a good woman like you slip through his fingers."

I was caught off guard by the comment. "Look, I like you and everything, but don't talk about him. I'm not trying to have him on my mind when I'm having fun with you. Aight?"

He nodded and took his phone out. "Smile for Snapchat." I stuck my tongue out, and he showed me the picture of me with the flowers around my head.

"I look cute," I said, smiling at the picture. He stood up.

"I gotta use the bathroom; I'll be right back." He walked up the stairs. I didn't think he was every coming back by how long he was gone.

I heard a bell chime, and noticed he left his phone on the table. I looked around before I picked it up. I threw it back down once I saw him coming down the stairs. I smiled when he walked up to me.

"I don't feel good at all; I don't know what they put in that drink, but I was just hurling upstairs. You want to just go back to my place and we can order something?"

I wasn't too sure about that, but he did look like he was about to throw up again.

"Ok; let's grab some Paella, and maybe you will feel better once you eat some, lightweight," I laughed, and he gave me a love tap on my thigh. We went and grabbed the food, and mad our way to his place in his car.

We pulled up to a tiny house surrounded by palm trees. It looked kind of shabby. I wished I would have brought my own car just in case something went wrong. I waited for him to open the door for me like Domo did, but he just stood at the gate and waited for me to get out. I was looking stupid as he looked at me. I opened the door and stepped out.

"You were waiting for an invitation or something?" he said laughing.

"No; my ex used to open the door and let me out."

He stopped laughing, and I could tell he didn't like me bringing Domo up because he just kept walking without responding. I walked behind him and he opened the door, and the inside was just as fucked up as the outside.

"This your place?" I said, looking at all the old furniture and shit that was scattered. I would have been embarrassed to bring anybody here.

"Let me grab you a plate." He went to the kitchen, and I could hear him clinking around.

"Can you bring a fork too!" I yelled loud enough for him to hear me.

"Aight!" he yelled back. He came in with a set of plates and forks. After he sat them down, he said he had to use the bathroom again, and he went all the way to the back. I could hear water running, which I thought was odd. I got up, and I could hear him talking a little through the vents. I pulled a chair under the vent and stood on it. I could hear him clear enough to make out what he was saying.

"Yeah, she here right now...damn Shay, you need to do something. This bitch starting to get on my nerves always talking about that bitch ass nigga Domo. You should have let me pop his has for what he did in that restaurant."

I jumped down and grabbed my purse. I open the door and ran out, hoping he didn't hear me. I pulled out my phone to call Domo.

"Hello."

It wasn't him; it must have been that broad from the mall.

"Put Domo on the phone," I said, speed-walking and out of breath.

"He in the shower; who is this calling my nigga?" she asked. This broad had me fucked up.

"This is wife, bitch; give him the fucking phone. He must ain't tell you I will put a cap in your ass if you keep fucking with me." I could hear her knocking on the door.

"Domo, you need to tell this bitch to have some respect," she said, yelling at Domo.

"Who you talking about?" he said, and I knew that tone. He had an attitude.

"She say she your wife; I don't give a fuck who the bitch—" she stopped talking and I heard a commotion.

"Bitch, call my wife out her name again and I will break it. What the fuck are you still doing here anyway? I told you to be gone before I got out the shower." I assumed he had her by the throat because I heard her coughing and gasping.

The phone hung up after he said that. Damn, he still went

hard for me. Fuck; I needed a damn ride, and I didn't know who else to call. I was about two blocks down from Jamal's place when Domo called back.

"Wassup Bella."

"Lashay set me up, Domo. I was out with Jamal tonight and he was on the phone with her, telling her I was here."

"Where you at, mami?"

I looked around at the street signs. "Ok, I'm at—" I stopped when I saw Jamal speed up the street and stop right beside me. I screamed.

"Bella, you ok?" I started running as fast as I could in my heels.

"He's chasing me, baby!" I screamed into the phone. I was running by people, and nobody even tried to help. I made the left in an alley, and hid in a shed behind somebody's house.

"Domo, I'm scared," I said, wishing I would have put my .22 in the purse.

"Baby, what street you on? Please tell me something."

I could hear footsteps. "Shhh, I think he outside," I said, trying to move further back. I thought the coast was clear. "It said Fellow Street."

The shed door came flying down, and I saw Jamal standing there looking like a psychopath.

"Come here, you little bitch!" he said, knocking shit out the way to get to me.

"Domo, help me!" I screamed.

"I love you, Baby; I'm on the way!" he screamed in the phone.

"He can't do shit to help you now," he said, snatching me up and clocking me in the head with something. I blacked out.

I woke up to water being thrown in my face. Lashay was sitting in a chair directly in front of me.

"Welcome back, sleepy head," she said, lighting a cigarette.

"You're one stupid bitch," I said, spitting at her. She slapped me across the face.

"No, you're the stupid bitch. You just couldn't sign the

papers and move on with your life? Jamal told me how you told him you never mailed them off. You acting so desperate to keep him," I laughed.

"I'm the desperate one? You think this is the first time I've been in a situation like this because of you dumb bitches who can't let the nigga go; you going to be just like her ass. Dead." She got up and put a knife to my throat. "Call Domo. "She said handing me the phone.

"No, call him yourself."

She hit me in the head with the butt of the knife. Jamal walked in the room and just looked at me with a smirk.

"You're mad at me, huh?" he said, laughing and walking to me.

"Go kill yourself, faggot."

He rubbed his hands together and kicked me out the chair, then stood over top of me.

"You know, even though this was just work, I been wanting to hit this pussy in the worst way," he said, rubbing his hand up my thigh.

"Jamal, get the fuck off of her. Thirsty ass nigga."

I could hear what sounded like a Facebook call. "Bitch, are you crazy?" I could hear Domo's voice through the phone. She turned it to me, and I was still on the ground.

"Bella, I'm coming baby." She turned her back to me.

"Still making empty promises, I see," she said, tapping the knife on her head.

"I just want to talk, Domo. I think you at least owe me that." She said sounding like she was about to cry.

"I don't owe you shit, Lashay. You either let Bella go, or you gonna wish you never woke up this morning."

She started laughing. "I thought you might feel like that," she said, nodding her head to Jamal. I heard a baby crying, and it sounded like DJ.. I looked up and saw Charlene walking in with DJ., and she looked like she got her ass whooped.

"Take the baby, Jamal," Lashay said.

"You better not touch my son, motherfucka," I said, trying

to get up. Lashay kicked me back down.

"Don't touch him," Charlene said, backing away.

"You scared, nigga!" Lashay said, walking over to Charlene and snatching DJ. out her arms. She handed Jamal the knife and he jammed it into Charlene's neck, and she grabbed the gash and fell.

"You see what happened to your aunty, lil' man?" Lashay said to DJ.. She turned the camera to Charlene's seemingly lifeless body.

"You bitch, I swear to God—" she cut him off.

"Yeah, I know. Catch me if you can, nigga!" she hung up, turned to Jamal, and nodded her head. She left out with DJ., and Jamal came to me with the knife.

"It's such a waste," he said, looking me over and rearing the knife back. As soon as he came down, he was knocked over and wasn't moving. I looked up, and Charlene was holding a wooden stick.

"Come on, Bella." She helped me up, but she was weak as hell.

"We need to go catch her." She sat on the couch holding her neck, which had blood pouring from it. She untied my hands.

"I'm gonna wait right here," she said like she was dozing off. I grabbed a rag off the floor and put it on her neck.

"You're gonna be ok. Give me your phone."

She handed it to me and laid her head back. I ran out the front of the house and called 911. I went to the mailbox to get the address. I told them to hurry because somebody was dying. I called Domo, and he answered right away.

"Charlene!" he yelled into the phone.

"No; it's me, baby. She took DJ.. Charlene is hurt bad." I started crying.

"I'm on the street you gave me earlier." I ran to the sidewalk since the street was only a couple blocks down.

"Keep driving up. I'm running down that way."

I saw his headlights, and I ran into the street waving my hands. He jumped out the car and ran to me. I fell into his arms and started bawling. Lando got out and walked up to us.

"Go help Charlene," I told him. I pointed to the house and he ran in.

"How we gonna get our baby back, Domo?"

He rubbed my back. "We're going to get him, baby. I promise" Domo said in an unsteady voice. I think I saw Satan himself when I thought about what I was going to do to her; I was sending that bitch straight to hell.

To be continued...

Made in United States
Cleveland, OH
07 June 2025

17548340R00073